# ACCENT ON MURDER

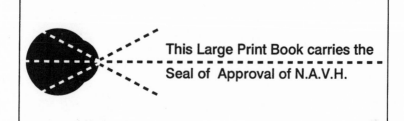

This Large Print Book carries the
Seal of Approval of N.A.V.H.

# ACCENT ON MURDER

**Richard and Frances Lockridge**

Thorndike Press • Thorndike, Maine

Thorndike Large Print ® Popular Series edition published in 1993 by arrangement with HarperCollins Publishers.

The tree indicium is a trademark of Thorndike Press.

This book is printed on acid-free, high opacity paper. ∞

Set in 16 pt. News Plantin by Minnie B. Raven.

---

**Library of Congress Cataloging in Publication Data**

Lockridge, Richard, 1898–
    Accent on murder : a Captain Heimrich mystery / by Richard and Frances Lockridge.
        p.  cm.
    ISBN 1-56054-301-9 (alk. paper : lg. print)
    1. Heimrich, M. L. (Fictitious character)—Fiction.  2. Police—New York (State)—Fiction.  3. Large type books.  I. Lockridge, Frances Louise Davis.  II. Title.
    [PS3523.O245A65  1993]
    813'.52—dc20                                        93-13220
                                                              CIP

---

# ACCENT ON MURDER

# I

Walter Brinkley, professor emeritus of English Literature at Dyckman University, typed to the bottom of page three hundred and fifty-two of "A Note on American Regional Accents" and decided that it devolved upon him to give a small party for Paul Craig and the new Mrs. Craig. The decision was so sudden, so apparently unmotivated, that Mr. Brinkley blinked slightly and re-read what he had just written, hoping to find explanation in typescript.

He was at once successful. He had been discussing — briefly, for four pages only — the subtle, and to so many nonexistent, difference in the pronunciation of the words "marry" and "Mary" and advancing, with appropriate reticence, certain theories as to regional customs in this connection. Mr. Brinkley was reticent because this was, after all, not actually his field. His field was Milton. His *Milton's Boyhood: Twelve to Sixteen* was, he did not doubt, a book which would stand. On regional accents he was, at best, an informed amateur. It was this fact which had led him to add "A Note on" to his earlier and tentative title

7

which, standing brazenly as "American Regional Accents," might have seemed presumptuous.

The word "marry" was, of course, the key word. Paul Craig had married, for the second time, almost a year before. But it was only now — only a week ago, at any rate — that he had brought his new wife home to the big Craig house in North Wellwood — the house which had been closed for so long that many of North Wellwood's newcomers regarded it rather as a monument to the past than as a residence of the present.

His young friend Craig was going to find things greatly changed, Walter Brinkley thought, separating the ribbon and carbon copies of page three hundred and fifty-two and placing them in their respective piles. Craig would not, probably, be pleased. His young friend Craig —

He must, Brinkley decided, quit thinking of Craig in that fashion. Paul Craig was — Brinkley made a quick computation — upward of fifty. Some years upward of fifty. And I, Walter Brinkley thought with that faint disbelief, that momentarily shadowing disappointment, which never failed to accompany such thoughts — I am sixty-seven. A doddering old man; a man turned out to pasture. Nevertheless, I will give a small cocktail party to welcome young Craig and his new wife.

Walter Brinkley thereupon bounced up from his typewriter — a rather short, comfortably round, noticeably brisk man, with thick and shining white hair and a little-lined pink face. He bounced out of his study, which was on the second floor of his white house on Hayride Lane, and bounced to the head of the stairs and said, down them, "Harry?"

Harry had been doing something — dusting, possibly — in the living room. He came out into the hall and looked up the stairs and said, "Yassuh. Yassuh, professor?"

How he loves the rôle, Walter Brinkley thought, crinkling inside but showing nothing — except good humor — in his face. The old family retainer; the faithful servant from the deepest South. What a game Harry Washington makes of it, without too much burlesque; without, Walter Brinkley thought, bitterness of any kind; how he plays a part for his amusement and — yes, that too — for mine. And he knows perfectly well that I know perfectly well he was born in New Jersey — South Jersey, admittedly — and went to public school there, and speaks, when he chooses to step out of character — as, for example, at meetings of the N.A.A.C.P. — precisely like anyone else born and educated in South Jersey. An interesting variant, the

South Jersey accent —

"Yassuh?" Harry Washington repeated, tolerantly. He was tall and lean and middling brown. He knew perfectly well what the professor was thinking. Every now and then the professor stopped, right in the middle of things, and thought. A very interesting man, the professor.

"Harry," Walter Brinkley said, "I've decided to give a party."

"A party?" Harry said, in honest astonishment. He corrected himself quickly. "A pahty?" he said.

That was a new one. Two or three people in to dinner — yes. A party, no. Not in the five years during which Harry had been Walter Brinkley's houseman. When Mrs. Brinkley had been alive — no doubt. But that was before his time.

"You means a real pahty, professor?" Harry said, partly to make sure and partly to get firmly back into the character from which, momentarily and in surprise, he had slipped.

"Cocktail party," Brinkley said. "For Mr. and Mrs. Craig. They've opened the big house."

"Sho nuff?" Harry said, rather overdoing it.

Harry knew quite well that Mr. Paul Craig had reopened the enormous brown-shingle house, with turrets no less, on Craig Lane. He knew that Mr. Craig had been married for about a year, and that he and his new wife had spent the ensuing time in journeying around the world; he knew that the new Mrs. Craig was a good many years — twenty, and more — younger than her husband, and that she was tall and slender and had black hair in tight curls (a real knockout, they said) and that she and her husband had brought a male cook (white) up with them and two maids, also white, and that Ellen White (who wasn't) was employed five days a week, six hours a day at a dollar seventy-five an hour, to do general cleaning, but that Joe Parks was being kept on as outdoor man and that Mrs. Joe Parks was expected to lend a hand as needed.

"You means that big brown house up toward Brewster?" Harry Washington said. "Great big old place? That's the place you means, professor?"

I must learn to be more exact, Walter Brinkley thought, and crinkled again inside.

"That's the place, Harry," he said, gravely. "The old Craig house."

"Oh," Harry said. "*That* house."

It's probably, Brinkley thought, because he slipped up on "party." He waited.

"When?" Harry said, and crinkled inside, also. And was externally grave, also.

11

"Let's see," Brinkley said. "Today's Tuesday."

"Nosuh," Harry said. "Wednesday, professor. Wednesday the eighteenth." He paused. "Of June," he added.

Walter Brinkley said, "Oh," not questioning it — Harry was always right in such matters. "Then — next Sunday?"

"Whatever you sez, professor."

So — not the next Sunday. Brinkley suggested Saturday, but without conviction. It was still whatever he said.

"All right, Harry," Walter Brinkley said. "When shall we give the party?"

"Whenever you sez, suh. Week from Saturday would be 'bout right. Time to invite people. Get me somebody to help — be twenty–thirty people likely —"

"Oh," Brinkley said, "I don't —"

"No suh," Harry said. "Thirty-five, probably."

Walter Brinkley had, a little vaguely, thought of a dozen or so. But, no doubt, Harry was right — he was always right in such matters, also. Brinkley remembered that in the old days — how saddening, yet, obscurely, how warming to think of the old days — parties had always turned out to be much larger than he, innocently, had expected. When one came — when Grace had come — to make a list — The warm sadness flowed over Walter Brinkley, who had loved his wife. He turned, without saying anything, and started to go back to his study, and now he did not bounce.

"Ice in the glass, professor," Harry said, and spoke very gently, so that the gentleness in his voice flowed too over Walter Brinkley. Brinkley swallowed and turned back.

"It's pretty near one o'clock, professor," Harry said. "Want I should mix it now? And's all right with you, suh, I thought maybe an omelet like. With creamed mushrooms? Cut a nice head of romaine this morning and it's good and crisp now, suh."

As gentle with me, Walter Brinkley thought, as if I were a child, not an old man, lonely in a house too large. He started down the stairs and for a moment Harry stood there, and looked up at him. Then Harry nodded his head once, as if he were satisfied, and Walter Brinkley nodded back, also once. Harry went off, then, to the kitchen, and Professor Brinkley — who much preferred to be called "Mr. Brinkley" but almost never was — went on down the stairs and across the hall and through the living room to the shady terrace beyond, and by the time he reached the terrace he was bouncing again.

Harry brought a martini in a little pitcher, with much ice, and a long-stemmed fragile glass, still frosty from the freezer for all the warmth of the early summer day, and poured into the glass quickly while the frost still held.

"Thank you, Harry," Brinkley said and Harry said, "Yassuh, professor. You makes yuh list, suh."

"Who," Margo Craig said, and held an invitation card in sight, "is Walter Brinkley? He wants us for cocktails on —" she looked at the card again — "a week from today."

It was Saturday afternoon, and the mail had just come, just been brought up from the rural-route box on Craig Lane, where the long, winding driveway from the big brown house — the big brown-shingled house, with turrets — joined the side road named after some generations of Craigs. The mail came late because the house was near the end of the mail driver's long route from the North Wellwood postoffice.

Margo Craig spoke with clarity, each word softly distinct — it was as if she found pleasure in the perfect formation of each word. But, as she sat on the awninged terrace of the big house — when she first saw the house two weeks ago she had thought, unexpectedly, of a great brown bear; ungainly, to some degree monstrous, but yet shaggily appealing — there was clarity in all of Margo Craig. A kind of special distinctness, Paul Craig thought, watching her.

Tall, slender, with long and stockingless legs, brown — a special brown where an intruding splinter of light touched them — from winter in the sun, she was very pleasant to look at. Paul Craig looked at her with approval, and he was a man who did not give approval lightly. Sitting in so low a chair, he thought, most women would seem to sprawl. Margo did not. Breeding, he thought, and that he had chosen wisely. It was appropriate that this young woman, immaculate of body and of mind, should, in a sense, have been appointed Craig.

"A professor of English," Paul Craig said. "Retired now, I think. The Brinkleys have been around here since the Revolution. Almost, indeed, as long as the Craigs. He spoke to me about the party the other day — yesterday or the day before — in the village. I gather that we are — rather the subjects of his party, my dear."

She said, "Oh?"

"A welcome back," Craig said. He was a tall, spare man, gray-haired; he wore slacks and a polo shirt, yet he seemed more formally clothed. He sat in a chair which, while certainly comfortable, was not essentially a terrace chair. It is difficult to achieve austerity

15

on a shaded terrace on a summer afternoon, particularly while sharing the terrace with a wife whose slim legs — revealed without indiscretion in walking shorts — are of quite disturbing symmetry, but Paul Craig did retain a certain austerity. He was not unconscious of Margo's pretty legs nor, indeed, of the rest of her — of her wide-eyed face, the delicate rise of her breasts under the (properly) loosely fitted shirt, of the delicate perfection of the fingers which held the invitation to cocktails at Walter Brinkley's house. He was proud of her; really, quite proud of her. He had been fortunate to find a second wife so suitable. She was more suitable, actually, than poor Helen had been. Helen, it had to be admitted, had been somewhat emotional; at times, even moody.

"I take it then," Margo Craig said, "that we go to Professor Brinkley's party?"

"I think so," Craig said. "It is, on the whole, thoughtful of Walter. A thoughtful gesture."

"I suppose," she said, "a rather — intellectual party?"

Craig smiled slightly, and sipped his drink and shook his head.

"I gather," he said, "people from around here, for the most part. Some of the people who've always been here — the Sands, the Farnleys, no doubt — and quite possibly some

16

of the — new arrivals."

"The ranch-house set?"

He smiled again, again slightly, and said that that, too, was quite possible. "Walter," he said, "is rather the gregarious type. He always was. Tolerant is perhaps the word. Or — unworldly."

She nodded and for a time neither said anything. Then she said, "I suppose the community has changed a great deal from — in recent years."

She had started to say "from the old days" and decided not to. Paul was not unduly sensitive about the difference in their ages — at least, he gave no indication of being — but he might find a certain connotation in "the old days."

He did not appear to notice that she had changed the wording of her sentence. He nodded; he said that the community had indeed. He said that the change was, he supposed, characteristic of all such communities as that which sprawled around North Wellwood Center.

"When I was growing up here," he said, "there were only the big houses. Like this one." He paused. "Well," he said, "perhaps not exactly like this one. Grandfather rather — let himself go when the old house burned down. Twenty acres — that was more or less

17

the minimum, probably. Now — two-acre plots. And — ranch types. Since it is possible — just possible, I'd be inclined to think — to commute by way of Brewster." He lighted a cigarette. "Progress, I imagine they call it," Paul Craig said, with rather marked detachment.

"No others?" she said, and he raised his eyebrows. "I mean," she said, "when you were growing up here. Farmers? People who worked on farms and — that sort of thing?"

"Oh," he said. "People like that — yes, of course. I wasn't thinking of them. There was even a place everybody called 'shack-town'. A rural slum, they would call it now, I suppose. I was thinking of the people we knew."

"Of course," she said, but now with only politeness in her voice. Then, "Are we swimming?"

Paul Craig swam very well. Like most people, he enjoyed doing what he did well. Margo Craig, in the eleven months of her life with Paul had noticed that, as she had noticed a good many things.

She was a small, quick girl; she had the deeply red hair of all the Camerons — hair so deeply, darkly red that a few women, not of generous nature, looked on it with skepticism, feeling that if valid it was outrageously unfair. She wore white shorts and a white shirt which had, for no special reason, a small green dragon embroidered above the breast pocket. She watched through an open window of the house on Hayride Lane and said, "He's even later than — there he is now," and said it to her cousin, and went out of the house and down the drive to get the mail.

Caroline Wilkins, who had been washing up after the late Saturday lunch, dried her hands and went to the door and watched her cousin go quickly, with something like exuberance, down the drive. As hopeful, of course (Caroline thought) of a letter from that Alan of hers as I of one from that Brady of mine. And then, somewhat irrelevantly, Damn the Navy anyway.

But Caroline Wilkins did not, of course, mean really to damn the Navy. One's family may well prove irritating, but one does not really damn one's family. Three years ago — no, going on four years ago — Caroline had married the Navy, in the person of Lieutenant Commander (then Lieutenant) Brady Wilkins. So now she was a Navy wife. But before that, and always — except for three months not to be counted, never to be remembered — she had been a Navy daughter — daughter of Vice Admiral Jonathan Bennett, USN (Ret.). She had been in China when she was four, and in Singapore when she was six, and in France from the time she was ten until she was twelve. There was always, for Navy families, much tentative perching on new branches. As, of course, now.

This particular perch was, to be sure, even more tentative than most. When Lieutenant Commander Brady Wilkins, USN (Annapolis, 1945; special courses at M.I.T., 1947–1948) had been transferred from Norfolk to the headquarters of Commander, Eastern Sea Frontier, 90 Church Street, New York City, a rented house in Northern Westchester had seemed a quite reasonable perch. She had assumed — they had both assumed — that for a couple of years (one planned no further ahead than that) Lieutenant Commander Wilkins would live a life reasonably like that of any other man who worked in a New York office and lived outside it. He might be expected to catch a train in and, most nights — when he did not have "the duty" — a train out.

It had not worked out that way; they should both have guessed it would not. Wilkins's assignment to Commander, Eastern Sea Frontier, turned out — as they might have expected — to be more subterfuge than fact; it was a place to hang up his pay account, his health record. It was a place at which the

Bureau of Naval Personnel could, officially, point a finger and say, "There he is." But there he seldom was. He was in Alaska, in Florida, in, as likely as not, London. That was what two intensive years at M.I.T. had done to Lieutenant Commander Wilkins — made him an always unpredictable migrant, veiled by security, most mysteriously employed.

And, the summer before, after they had rented a white house on Hayride Lane and moved into it, this had led Caroline to feel herself almost as much Navy widow as Navy wife. "For the next while," Brady told her one evening, on the terrace — "for the next quite a while, I'll be here and there. If you're going to stay here, you'd better get somebody to stay with you. Dorcas?"

And Dorcas — Cousin Dorcas, Dorcas Cameron, daughter of Caroline's Aunt Dorcas Cameron — it had turned out to be; turned out, on the whole, most satisfactorily to be. Four years younger, which had seemed a span a dozen years ago, and seemed a snap of the fingers now; destined, it now appeared, to rejoin the Navy community from which her mother had seceded — if the Navy would let Lieutenant Alan Kelley light long enough; small and quick and gay, with burnished hair; by her own, slightly rueful, statement "cute." "You're beautiful," Dorcas had said when

21

they were discussing such matters. "I'm —
cute." But that was not, Caroline thought
now, looking down the driveway toward Hayride Lane, fair to Dorcas. The term diminished Dorcas.

Dorcas, at the mailbox, looked toward the
house, and held her right arm up and waggled
something white in her right hand. So he had;
at any rate, one of them had. Dorcas came
up the driveway from Hayride Lane with a
considerable collection of mail under her arm,
and something slipped out of the collection
and lay, small and white, on the gravel.
"Hey!" Caroline called from the door, and
pointed, and Dorcas stopped and said, "Oh,"
and went back for the something white.

She came on — quick; there was commonly
something of a trot even in Dorcas's less hurried movements — and dumped mail on a coffee table in the living room. She said, "Here
it is," and held an envelope out and said, in
the same breath, "Mine didn't, the bum," and
shuffled through the rest of the mail, leaving
Caroline to hers. Most of it was what they
dismissed as "trash-can stuff." Part of it was
the weekend edition of the *North Wellwood
Advertiser* and part the (rather fragile) Saturday edition of the *New York Herald Tribune*.

There was also — and it was that which
had slipped away and been reclaimed — a

small envelope; an invitation envelope. Its inadequate surface was crowded with address:

> Cdr. and Mrs. Brady Wilkins,
> Miss Dorcas Cameron,
> RFD 1,
> North Wellwood, New York.

"Glory be to God that there are no more of us," Dorcas sang — soundlessly — to herself and opened the little envelope. Then she said, "Why, the old dear," this time audibly, but when she looked at her cousin she saw that Caroline had something more important to listen to. So she waited until Caroline had finished listening to the far away (she supposed; he usually was) voice of Lieutenant Commander Brady Wilkins, assigned to an operation apparently too secret to have a name; now — she had allowed herself to look at the postmark — in San Diego, but probably *by* now, by this Saturday afternoon, somewhere else.

Caroline finished her husband's letter, but held it, still, in both hands in her lap. She's far away, Dorcas thought — so far away. Do I look like that when I read a letter Alan has written, listen to Alan's voice? Not quite like that, of course. With us it is — it's tomorrow, or the day after. And with them it's now — complete.

Caroline looked at her.

"How's your sailor?" Dorcas said. "Home from the sea?"

She was very matter of fact, very casual.

"Seems to be fine," Caroline said. "Might even —" She was matter of fact, too. But her voice, for all that, wavered a little. "Might even honor us," she said. "Next weekend, even. If something he can't mention happens to something he can't write about at a place which shall be forever nameless."

Then she raised eyebrows, enquiring.

"Not a line," Dorcas said. "Not an everloving line. Or any other kind. I —"

"Well," Caroline said, "after all, it's only been three days. And if it is sea duty it'll probably be 'proceed and report,' maybe even with 'to count as leave' thrown in." Caroline, twenty-six, three years married, looked at her cousin — twenty-two, marriage arranged for whenever the United States Navy decided, in its wisdom, it could spare Lieutenant Alan Kelley long enough. How the child's eyes shine at that, "to count as leave," Caroline thought, and said, "The rest for the ash can?"

"Pretty much —" Dorcas said, and then said, "No. The sweet old thing's giving a party," and held out the invitation from the sweet old thing — an appellation which would

24

have pleased Walter Brinkley, Ph.D. had he known of it.

"Cocktails, five to eight," Caroline read, and, "June twenty-eighth" and "RSVP."

"The lamb," Caroline said.

They had known the sweet old thing for less than a year; for most of the time they had shared the house on Hayride Lane half a mile or so north of the "old Brinkley place"; a house just (for Dorcas) within commuting distance of an editorial assistant's desk in the city; a house where Navy wives (present and to come) could hold each other's hands against emptiness. (And keep a shotgun handy to frighten away marauders, who had not appeared.)

Professor Brinkley had waved at them, quite as if he had known them for some time, the previous autumn — a glowing yellow day in autumn — as he was fishing mail from his rural box and they were driving past in an open car. After that, they had asked him to tea — which had seemed a suitable beverage for a white-haired, retired professor — and Walter Brinkley had drunk it without protest. But during the Christmas holidays — when it is especially dreary to be alone; Brady Wilkins had been, mysteriously as always, in Alaska — "the sweet old thing," known alternatively as "the lamb," had invited them down, also for "tea." He had, however, said, "If you really like the stuff," after which matters proceeded in more conventional paths.

"Neighbors?" Dorcas said, and Caroline raised slim shoulders under the fleece of a summer sweater.

"Of course," she said, "it could be more professors."

"From the sample," Dorcas said, "professors seem very nice. Woolly."

At the barracks of Troop K, Hawthorne, New York, invitation envelopes are infrequent, the mail consisting of what are known as "squeals," which are often rambling and seldom short, and official communications which seldom have to do with the more cheerful aspects of everyday life — such as, for example, cocktail parties. But the small envelope addressed to "Captain M. L. Heimrich, BCI, State Police Barracks, Hawthorne, N. Y." did, dutifully find its way into the proper "In" basket, where it was quickly buried under bulkier papers. Captain Heimrich is, however, a man prone to get to the bottom of things, even of "In" baskets, and in due time he found that he was invited to have cocktails with one Walter Brinkley, in Wellwood.

This did not, immediately, convey anything

to Heimrich, who closed his eyes better to consider. There was a "Brinkley" — something very like Brinkley, at any rate — who had been sent up for aggravated assault. It seemed improbable that he would request the pleasure of Captain Heimrich's presence at any function which did not involve blackjacks. There was a "Brinkley" — no, that was more like Barkly — who thought he had invented a new method to kill a wife, and found himself mistaken. Not this Brinkley, obviously. This Brinkley —

Heimrich was shaking his head when he remembered. A round engaging man, pink of face, white of hair and, as recalled, worried of expression. A man who had been meticulous; who had spoken of the indeterminate sound of a vowel and so, somewhat abruptly, brought a brief investigation to an acceptable end. *Professor* Walter Brinkley. That was the man.

It is always difficult for a detective, and especially one concerned primarily with homicide, to "RSVP" with any confidence. People kill other people at cocktail hour, as at other times; on Saturdays as on other days.

On the other hand — although why he thought of it in that way was not entirely clear — a gray-eyed young woman named Susan Faye would, on the Saturday in question, be driving a grave-eyed boy named Michael to summer camp. (There would be a mournful big dog in the car.) She, therefore, would not be available. So — if murderers would refrain from murdering, naturally — it might be pleasant to see Professor Brinkley again, with nothing hanging on vowels, determinate or indeterminate.

# II

It was surprising, Walter Brinkley thought at four-thirty on the afternoon of Saturday, June twenty-eighth, how one guest led to another. It had been different in the old days; it had been, "They'll start coming in about an hour, dear, so don't you think —" in the gentlest, the dearest remembered, of voices. It had been, "You will remember to be especially nice to poor dear Thelma, won't you, Walter?" But then too there had, usually, been more people than he would have expected, and now, more clearly than before, he understood why. It was, specifically, that one guest did lead to another.

The Sands, of course. And the Farnleys. And Jerry Hopkins — the cantankerous old galoot. But if the Sands, then, if one was not to be rude, the Abernathys, who went around so much with the Sands. And if the Abernathys, the Thayers, also, since he knew the Thayers equally well, and had known them for as long a time. And dear old Mrs. Belsen — who was really a person one invited to tea, instead of to cocktails — would be surprised, and in her gentle way might even be hurt, if other old-timers, like the Farnleys, for example, were invited and she was not. Mrs. Belsen, of course, led inevitably to the Misses Monroe, listed in telephone directory as "Monroe, Misses, the," a form which had always delighted Walter Brinkley. And since the party was, after all, for young Craig (How boyhood habits of thought do linger!) it would be unpardonable to omit the Knights, although Walter did not, himself, much care for Jasper Knight. (There had been the matter, while it was Jasper's turn, in the methodical revolution of Republican wheels, to be town supervisor, of the exemption from two-acre zoning of a considerable area of land, almost all of which had happened to be the property of Jasper Knight.) I must, Walter Brinkley thought, a little worriedly, try not to be prejudiced against Republicans.

Brinkley adjusted his blue bow tie, knowing that long before the party was over it would have ceased to pursue the even tenor of its ways, and that he would not remember to do anything about it, and went downstairs to ask about the ice.

Harry Washington wore a white coat which shone. He said, "Now jes rest yuhself, professor," and that the ice — a big bag of the ice — was in the freezer. He said, also, that Ellen White, available since she did not work on Saturdays for the Craigs, would be there in plenty of time to pass the canapés, and that the inn *had* sent the canapés, and that Ben had been instructed about parking the cars, and that the bar was all set up and that there would be plenty of liquor, of all kinds, to go around — and around and around and around, if the younger set, the "ranch-house set," felt like revolving.

"I make it forty-three," Walter Brinkley said. "Will there be room enough, Harry?"

" 'Ceptin around the bah," Harry said. "Now you jes rest yuhself, professor. Only it's forty-five if Mister and Miz Sands bring their weekend guests, like they said maybe."

Walter Brinkley went out onto the terrace, and sat in a shady place, and was very glad that the afternoon was fine, because that meant that the party could, if it chose, spill over onto the terrace. It meant also, which is always important at country parties, that cars, which would necessarily be parked off the driveway, on the lawn, would not be mired there. Sometimes guests kept coming back for days, often with tow trucks, and what the turf looked like afterward —

I, Walter Brinkley thought, am getting so that I worry about not having to worry about things. A doddering old man — too old for this sort of thing. A fussy old man, anticipating

31

dire consequences from the most innocent of things. What, really, could go wrong at a small party — and with Harry to see to things — on a pleasant afternoon in early summer? Jes rest yuhself, professor. And what part of the Deep South did Harry fancy his assumed, his so carefully assumed, accent came from? Professor Brinkley ran it over in his mind. Georgia? Not quite Georgia. Tennessee, then? Perhaps a little nearer Tennessee. It would be interesting to know where Harry's parents had grown up since it must have been from them Harry mimicked the soft accents he used — when he remembered to — for, surely, his own amusement. Or, gently to ridicule — without hatred, conceivably to avoid hatred — the paler skinned ones he, and all his color, had cause to hate?

A car — the most ancient of Rolls-Royces, with the most ancient of men driving it — crept cautiously off Hayride Lane, into the driveway. That would be the Misses Monroe. They would be surprised, fluttered, to be first. They had so been fluttered since he could remember, Walter Brinkley thought, and crinkled inside, and walked across the terrace, toward the drive, to greet his guests.

Lieutenant Commander Brady Wilkins had been in San Diego and then he had been in

Texas — what was the Navy doing in Texas? — and then in Florida, at Key West, where it might be that the Navy was doing a variety of things. And now he was either in New York, probably at 90 Church Street, or — *on his way to North Wellwood.* They had been on the terrace, finishing lunch, when the telephone rang inside and, very quickly, Caroline said, "I'll take it," and spoke with a kind of excitement in her voice. She went through the open french doors; Dorcas could hear her steps — so much quicker than usual; it was almost as if she were running — on the wide boards of the living room floor. And, tensed too, listening, Dorcas found that she was holding her breath — holding her breath for Caroline, hoping for Caroline.

"Hello," she heard Caroline say, and the ordinary word seemed somehow to tremble. But then Caroline said, "Oh. *Darling,*" and Dorcas got out of the terrace chair and walked off on the lawn until she had walked away from her cousin's voice — from the eagerness, the happiness in a voice which belonged to only two and was nothing to be spied upon. I'm so glad, Dorcas Cameron thought; so glad for her.

She did not return quickly to the terrace; did not return at all, indeed, until Caroline stood on the terrace, in the sun, with the sun on her honey-colored hair, and looked toward her across the sweep of green and then moved her head in a gesture which beckoned. Dorcas went back, then, and went quickly, and did not need to be told, because her cousin's face was lighted with it, and was told anyway.

"Brady," Caroline said. "In New York. And — coming up. This afternoon. Borrowing a car and —"

"Darling," Dorcas said and then, "It's wonderful" and then, "I'm so glad," and took the hands Caroline held out to her. And then, rather absurdly, very delightedly, the two girls did a little circling dance on the terrace, in the sunlight.

There was, however, more to it. Lieutenant Commander Brady Wilkins was in New York, was coming up. However —

When he would get there depended on things which he could not entirely control; on, it appeared — and, as always, appeared in the murk of security — a man he had to see in regard to something he wasn't supposed to mention. (And wouldn't mention, even to a wife; even to a wife who was also Caroline.) If he and this man could finish with what they had to discuss early enough, Brady Wilkins would be in time for the party. To "drop in on the party."

"I don't," Caroline said, "think he'll want

to stay long. Or — that either of us will."

"I should think not," Dorcas said.

"So much to — that is, to talk about," Caroline said.

"I," Dorcas said, and spoke gravely, while laughter, and delight, flickered in her eyes, "would think there might be."

To which Caroline said, of course, *"You!"*

It was four-thirty, and Dorcas was under a shower, changing for the party when, faintly over the sound of beating water, she heard the telephone ring again. She shut the water off and was wrapping herself in a towel robe, but then the telephone was stopped in the middle of its ringing, so she wriggled in the robe to dry her body and stood on first one foot and then the other to dry brown feet and legs. She was, she decided, getting a good start; was well along to browning, although it still was June. That was because they had "the place" — the place they had found early the previous autumn, too late in the year to do much good, but a place which had been wonderful, now, since mid-May.

It was a sheltered place — a kind of cup of sunlight, some distance from the house, with the house, and a dip of ground, and many trees and bushes between it and the road. It was smooth grass, shielded alike from breeze and from alien observation, and a wonderful place for sun-bathing. It might have been planned for that — dry under the robe, walking along the hallway from her bedroom toward the much larger "master" bedroom, so commonly without any "master" — Dorcas wondered if it had. She said, "Hi?" tentatively, into the large bedroom.

"Brady," Caroline said, and turned on the padded bench in front of her dressing table. Caroline was brown too; browner, if anything, thanks to their "solarium." "He's just leaving."

"Oh," Dorcas said, and the tone was a little flat.

"Yes," Caroline said. "And — two hours, with weekend traffic. At least two hours."

To which Dorcas again said, "Oh."

"So," Caroline said, "you go along when you want to and we'll come when we can. Sevenish, probably."

"You will?" She looked at the brown-all-over of "the beautiful one" and thought of Brady Wilkins and was, somewhat, inclined to doubt it.

"*You*," Caroline said. "Of course we will. For a quick one, anyway. We promised the lamb."

So, at a little after five — there was no use twiddling thumbs about it — Dorcas Cameron called, "Be seeing you," upstairs to her cousin, and went across the terrace toward the garage — went the long way around, by path, because grass will, when one least expects it, stain white shoes. She wore a green linen dress and went hatless. It was not until she was turning into the Brinkley driveway in the little commuting Ford that it occurred to her that this might be one of those at which people wore hats. And, it was even conceivable, white gloves.

Nonsense, Dorcas Cameron decided and said, "Hello, Ben," to the elderly colored man in white jacket who had said, "Afternoon, Miss Cameron," and waited to do something with her car. "Treat her gently, Ben," Dorcas said, "she's pretty feeble," and Ben laughed at that — what gaiety there is in their laughter, Dorcas thought — and said, "Sho will, Miss Cameron." And then she went to the door, at which the lamb — the lamb himself — waited.

"My dear," William Brinkley said, as if he meant it, and then, "No cousin?"

She explained. Looking into the big, cool living room, she said, "I guess I'm early, Mr. Brinkley." She had heard about the professor part — that it was an appellation for the campus. "Of course not," he said, "come and meet the Misses Monroe."

The Misses Monroe did wear hats — little

white hats, with flowers. They were not identical white hats, but they were very sisterly white hats. Each Miss Monroe wore a white glove on her left hand, and cuddled another white glove within it. The Misses Monroe were much of a size, which was small, and they had faces which reminded Dorcas of soft pink tissue paper, ever so tenderly crumpled. They wore silk dresses, and one of the dresses was gray with a print of very tiny yellow flowers and the other was pale blue with very tiny white flowers. One of the Misses Monroe was Miss Elvina and the other was Miss Martha.

"Such a pretty little neighbor, Walter," Miss Elvina said, when Brinkley had introduced them. "So pretty," Miss Martha said. But already, Dorcas was not entirely sure which was Miss Elvina and which Miss Martha. "We're always the first," Miss Martha (or Elvina) said and Miss Elvina (Miss Martha?) said, "Always. I can't think why. But we always are, aren't we, Walter?"

"So much the better, Martha," Walter Brinkley said, and moved a chair needlessly, but indicatively, for Dorcas and, when she was in it, sat on the sofa beside the Misses Monroe. He sat on the edge of the sofa, prepared to bounce.

"The old Adams house," Miss Elvina (it had to be Elvina) said, and Dorcas smiled and looked at her, and had not the faintest idea what she was talking about.

"Where you and Caroline live," Walter Brinkley said. "The last time an Adams lived in it was fifty years ago."

"Walter," Miss Martha said, as if about to tap him with a fan. "You're making fun again."

"And it's not," Miss Elvina said, unexpectedly, "as if you were a spring chicken, Walter."

"It's his having been away so much," Miss Martha said. "In New York." She spoke, Dorcas thought, as if New York, fifty-odd miles down the Harlem Division of the New York Central were some place incredibly remote.

"And London," Miss Elvina said. It was odd, Dorcas thought, how much nearer, for some reason, London sounded in the gentle, aging voice. They both looked at her; then they looked at each other.

"So nice young people are coming back," Miss Martha said, and Miss Elvina said, "So very nice." "You know," Miss Martha said, "somehow she reminds me of dear Gertrude. When we were all girls. The hair?"

"Gertrude had brown hair," Miss Elvina said. "But I see what you mean, dear. There comes Jerry Hopkins, Walter." Miss Elvina was, Dorcas realized, sitting so that she could look through a window toward the driveway. "In that funny little red car."

"Matches his complexion," Miss Martha said, but without malice.

Walter Brinkley stood up, then. A pretty, dark-brown girl in a green uniform went to the front door. And Harry Washington came with a tray with a frosty glass on it, and said, "A daiquiri, Miss Cameron? Seems like I remembers." He did.

"And," Miss Elvina said, "those new people from the old Mansfield place."

"The new people, Elvina," Walter Brinkley said, "have lived in the Mansfield place for over a dozen years."

"You're making fun again," Miss Martha said. "Don't mind him, Miss Cameron. Your cousin's Navy, isn't she?"

"Yes," Dorcas said. "She's —"

"Mr. Hopkins," Walter Brinkley said. "Jerry Hopkins. This is Miss Cameron, Jerry."

"The old Adams place," Jerry Hopkins said. He was short and wide and, as promised, red of face; he spoke somewhat hoarsely, but with vigor. He said, "Elvina. Martha." He said, "Short scotch, Harry."

"The Adamses were Navy people," Miss Elvina said.

"Army," Miss Martha said.

"I'm almost sure, Navy," Miss Elvina said. "But, it really comes to the same thing, doesn't it?"

"Well —" Dorcas said, and then Walter Brinkley touched her gently on the shoulder and said, "Some people'd like to meet you." She stood up and smiled at the Misses Monroe, and, guided, moved with him a little way into the room — the room which, very rapidly, had begun to fill.

"They're sweet," she said.

"Yes," Walter Brinkley said. "There's never been anything to sour them, of course." He had been guiding her toward the bar, toward, she supposed, introductions to those now clustered at the bar. (There was, Dorcas decided, *a* time to come to the party; a time everybody — except the Misses Monroe; herself — came.) Brinkley stopped and she stopped with him. He said, "Of course. Indiana." She smiled and shook her head, not in negation, but to show herself for the moment lost. "Say something," he told her. She raised eyebrows. "Anything," he said. "Say, 'What am I doing here among all these old people?'"

"All right," she said, and said it. "But that isn't the way I feel," she added.

"Southern part of the state," he said. "Not

extreme south. But nearer Kentucky than the lake."

"Oh," she said. "Where I come from? Yes." There was a little puzzlement in her voice.

"I'm sorry, my dear," Brinkley said, but did not at all speak sorrowfully; spoke rather as if he were pleased. "A wretched, intrusive habit of mine. I've fallen into bad hobbies."

"Oh," she said. "The way I speak. It's so evident? But I went to school in the East."

"Smith," he told her, accurately. "You must forgive a puttering old man." He blinked slightly. "Professor," he added, with distaste. "Yes, Elvina and Martha are sweet old things. Their grandfathers — both of them — made a great deal of money. The Monroe house on Main Street has twenty-three rooms. For two little old ladies. Past presidents of the garden club, of course."

"And," she said, "arbiters?"

She pleased him. His pleasant pink face told her that. He chuckled to tell her that.

"Arbiters emeritus," he said. "I'm afraid most of us are, in our various fashions. Emeritus, I mean. Let's find you some of the younger ones. *And* a drink."

Her glass was empty. There were younger ones. (The younger ones seemed to be, also, the later ones.) By six there were a good many people — in the room, on the terrace; younger

42

ones and older ones and those in between. They had names that flickered into the mind and flickered out of it — out, at any rate, of hers. There were people called Sands and people called Farnley. There was a Mrs. Belsen, who was rather taller than six feet, and had a tiny voice — tiny and distant, so that Dorcas felt herself stand on tiptoe to listen. There were Thayers and Abernathys and some people named Craig. (Scotch-and-plain-water people, most of them.) The Craigs — she was much younger than he and a little, somehow, more urban — had, Dorcas gathered, been away for some time and were, in a sense, being greeted. Possibly, to a degree at any rate, the party was being given "for" them, although this was not ever specifically made clear. There was, as there always was, a young man with that Where-have-you-been-all-this-time? look in his eyes, although he said nothing so obvious, and he was pleasant. And, after a time, forgettable.

There was, in short, the uneventful, friendly blur of any cocktail party — the blur of people met and parted from; of conversations begun and almost at once ended, of words overheard and almost at once forgotten, of groups which formed only to dissolve and to re-form. Walter Brinkley, she realized, had, especially during the first half of the party

— the time up to and including equilibrium: that moment when it was apparent that most of those who were coming had come and those who were leaving early had not yet begun to leave — unobtrusively kept the groupings fluid.

It was true that, along toward seven — by which time Dorcas had almost given up on Caroline and Brady Wilkins — a certain pattern did develop. The party tended to divide itself between terrace and living room, and it was, generally, true that the division was by age groups, with the younger — the "ranch-house set" — on the terrace and the older — the "emeritus set" — inside. But the Craigs were inside, and she, at any rate, was young. And Walter Brinkley was back and forth, and seemed adaptable to both groups although, Dorcas realized, professors do not retire before sixty-five or so. (Really, a woolly lamb, Dorcas thought.)

The Misses Monroe fluttered away, in the antique Rolls, almost precisely at seven. This was one of those meaningless things Dorcas remembered afterward, when she tried to remember things with meaning, although with no assurance that meaning lay in anything which had happened at Walter Brinkley's party.

It was after the Misses Monroe had gone

that, inside, near the bar, she found herself part of a group which included a middle-aged couple who looked only vaguely familiar, and turned out to be the Thayers, and Brinkley and a solid man with a square face — a face which appeared to have been carved from some dark wood.

"On my hobbyhorse again, my dear," Walter Brinkley said, and held her arm lightly. "Oh — this is Captain Heimrich. He's a cop." The word "cop" sounded, just perceptibly, as if Brinkley's mind put marks of quotation around it.

"No," Brinkley said, "I don't say I could do that. Not as well as he did." He broke off, turned to include her. "We're talking about a man on the radio," he said. "Years ago. When you must have been in pigtails, or whatever the modern counterpart is. A man who could tell, most of the time, what part of the country people came from, sometimes down to quite special areas, by hearing them talk. A parlor trick, in a way, but he was good at it. I was just telling the captain here that the game wasn't — fixed. Skeptical men, policemen."

"Now Mr. Brinkley," the man named Heimrich said, detached, pleasantly amused. He had very blue eyes.

"And," Brinkley said, "that an especially

45

acute ear is necessary. An ear more acute than mine. But that the differences are there, if one can hear them. Even when people try to hide them. Cover them up."

"He," Dorcas told the others, "spotted my home state. And the school I went to."

"Only today," he said. "After hearing you speak rather often. And, Indiana is quite easy. Even with an overlay. This radio man could do it in minutes."

"I," Mrs. Thayer said, "can't tell that she speaks differently from anyone else. Probably, Walter, you were merely lucky."

"Say 'drawing,' " Brinkley told her.

"I certainly shall not," Mrs. Thayer — she was gray-haired, had a golfer's complexion, was firm of voice. "I shall do nothing to encourage you, Walter."

"Say 'It would be merry to marry Mary,' " he told her.

"What a ridiculous thing to say," Mrs. Thayer said. "Pay no attention to him, Miss Cameron. He's a phoneticist."

"Emeritus," Brinkley said. "You do make it sound bad, Hilda. I —"

He was interrupted. A tall, gray-haired man, a man with a long face — oh, of course, Mr. Craig — made the interrupting sound, a tentative clearing of the throat. He was standing beyond a slender black-haired woman who had her back to them — oh, yes, Mrs. Craig. Walter Brinkley, indicating that he was listening, listened.

"Walter," Craig said, "I'm sorry — we're both sorry. But —"

Brinkley, Dorcas thought, looked a little surprised, and then at once regretful, with a host's regret.

"The fact is," Craig said, "Margo's come up with a headache. Thinks I'd better take her home."

Brinkley said, "Oh," and that he was sorry and moved out of the group to say something to Margo Craig which Dorcas — moving away herself, since the group was broken — could not hear. Mrs. Craig shook her head and then Brinkley went with the Craigs across the room toward the door.

"A delightful party," the solid man said, filling a pause, standing beside Dorcas. He was, she realized, taller than she had thought — his solidity somehow masked his height. The policeman, the "cop." It was a little odd, she thought without really thinking about it at all, that Professor Brinkley should know a policeman. The policeman smiled down at her, not asking a reply to a remark obviously meaningless — a remark made to fill a pause. There was, however, something companionable about his smile. "Too bad to have a headache in the middle of it," he said.

"The poor thing," she said, and they both moved away from the bar, to let other people move to the bar.

They moved toward the front of the room, where the people were fewer — together, but not in any real sense, together.

"A —" Heimrich began and stopped, because the girl was not listening, was looking through the window — the wide window at the front of the living room. A Cadillac came up, and Ben got out of it and went around it and held the door open, and Mrs. Craig got in. Craig gave him something and Ben smiled and nodded and Craig got in on the other side and the big car moved off. But when it had completed half a turn, it stopped so that an open car could come through, and in behind it. Then the Cadillac pulled away.

"Oh," Dorcas said. "They finally —" And then, in quite another tone, she said, "*Oh!*" again, and moved toward the door, forgetting Captain M. L. Heimrich. A pretty thing, Heimrich thought. And who does she see?

She saw, obviously, a young woman with honey-colored hair, in a white dress, and a tall, black-haired man in slacks and a sports jacket and another man — not so tall, wiry, with sandy hair. They were getting out of the open car. It was they — one of them, at any

48

event — that the pretty little girl with red hair was hurrying to meet. A polite little girl, well brought up, in too much of a hurry to say goodbye.

The sandy-haired man was the one she hurried to, Heimrich saw. They look fine together, he thought.

"Captain," Hilda Thayer said, coming up behind him, touching his arm. "Do you really catch murderers?"

# III

A pleasant party, Heimrich thought, driving away from the remnants of it at a few minutes before eight — driving toward the setting sun, toward the other side of Westchester County, toward his room at the Old Stone Inn in Van Brunt, which recently he had found a convenient place to live when he was not compelled by circumstances to bunk down in the Troop K barracks. Some of the new and some of the old at the party.

He thought of the Misses Monroe and smiled and shook his head a little. In another few years, he thought, there would be no more Misses Monroe. Not anywhere. And, although the houses might stand for years yet — stand until they burned down, which is the expectable final fate of frame houses — there would be no more of the big white houses, either. It would not matter if the houses stood for a long time yet, some of them — this was particularly true across the line in near Connecticut — with Revolutionary cannon balls embedded in ancient timbers. They would, if they did not burn down first (and if zoning authorities permitted, as after much fussing

50

they usually did) be converted into multiple family dwellings. The old white houses on the many Main Streets.

State troopers rode horses in those days, he thought. The distance he would drive from North Wellwood to Van Brunt in an hour or so must have taken a long time on a horse. On the other hand, there must have been much less need to hurry in those old days — fewer people must have meant fewer crimes. Not, he supposed, that the people in the big white houses were essentially more law abiding than those in the new, often vari-colored, ranch houses, "contemporary" houses. They might even have been inclined to take things into their own hands; the grandfathers of the Misses Monroe had certainly taken a good deal into theirs, and with fewer restrictions on the taking. Which might, one would suppose, have conditioned them to accept, in general, fewer restrictions on everything.

In another few years, he thought — having nothing else of special interest to think about — there will be no more mixtures of the old and the new such as had made Professor Brinkley's party gently interesting. (He could not contend that it had been wildly exciting.) The pretty girl with the dark red hair — she and her cousin and her cousin's husband and the sandy-haired young man she had gone with such innocently revealed eagerness to meet — they and their friends would take over. (Of course, they were not really of the "ranch-house set." They were Navy, which made a difference. But everybody was something, which made a difference too.)

The Misses Monroe and, no less, the Brinkleys, the Thayers, the other big-white-house people, wouldn't be around much longer. Which, Heimrich thought, is true everywhere, of course. Except that here, in Northern Westchester, in Northern Fairfield, too, there is a more immediate overlapping than in many places, so that one can see more clearly what is going on — see the old, the rural, dissolving in the strong solvent of the new, the semi-urban. (Well, then, the "exurban.")

The Misses Monroe, the Mrs. Belsens, did not, he supposed, following the meandering blacktop beyond Katonah, toward Yorktown Heights, realize in any real sense that this final change was going on. (There were still presidents of garden clubs, who still wore hats, usually, and appropriately enough, with flowers on them.) Oh, they knew, of course — by and large, in his considerable experience, they were observant and intelligent people. But they did not *feel* the change they saw; did not really believe in it.

The Professor Brinkleys, of course, both

knew and felt. But there were not many Professor Brinkleys, who were of "the big-white-house set" more or less by chance; who might have come from, lived, anywhere. (Except, as the professor himself would have been the first — very much the first — to point out, for a matter of accent. How he did ride that hobby! And, to be fair, how interesting he made it!) And the Craigs — the Craigs felt it strongly enough, and tried to hold it back. They tried to hold it back not only on the material level — with zoning laws, with stratagems to maintain what they so commonly called the "rural character" of such areas as they preferred to keep to themselves. They tried to hold it back on the more subtle, seldom openly admitted, basis of class.

Heimrich wondered, idly, whether it had not been the presence, at the professor's party, of so many of the ranch-house set, *commuters,* which had given that pretty Mrs. Craig her sudden headache. Or — and at this thought he grinned to himself — the presence of so clearly a lower class individual as a policeman.

Craig. Hadn't he heard something about a Craig? A Paul Craig?

Idly, for want of anything better to do, Heimrich upped the cards of that mental filing cabinet all good policemen maintain. "Craig." No, no Craig. Not anything, then, with which he had had to do directly. Something he had heard about. Therefore, not in the filing cabinet. If anywhere, in the catchall of loose ends.

It remained vague, without outlines. He did not worry it; it was not worth worrying. Something — wasn't it? — about the rather unforgiving attitude Craig had taken toward someone — an employee? — who had done some small thing another man might have passed over, not called the cops about. "There's a mean bastard for you" — hadn't someone said that about a man named Craig, after quite correctly listening to Craig, quite properly taking the steps indicated? Possibly — something like that. The outlines did not appear. No problem of mine, Heimrich thought; no problem then or now.

He had a late dinner at the Old Stone Inn. He walked, in the evening's coolness, for a time in Van Brunt Center. He went back to the Old Stone Inn and went to bed.

"I," Lieutenant Alan Kelley — USN, but momentarily in sports jacket and slacks — said across the table, "should very much like to marry for money. In fact, I was brought up to expect it. It is an old Annapolis tradition and I am an old Annapolis grad, steeped in tradition."

" 'Grad' indeed," Dorcas said.

They had reached coffee and cigarettes. To celebrate, they had also reached tiny glasses of cognac. They were at a table for two under a bust of, Dorcas thought, Hermes. But, perhaps, Apollo; one Greek god looks very like another. They were in a restaurant in Ridgefield.

"Then," Dorcas said, "you will have to look farther. Much farther."

"Don't think I haven't," Alan told her. "Over and above the call of."

"I'm sure of it," she said. "I don't doubt it for a moment. It's really 'proceed and report'? And 'to count as leave'?"

"Commander, Atlantic Fleet, for service aboard DD 197. 15 July. To count as leave. You keep changing the subject."

"For how long?"

He touched her hand. He shook his head. He said, "Now baby." He said, "You keep changing the subject."

"Money," she said. "I still haven't got any."

He managed to look extremely sad. He shook his head very sadly.

"And otherwise," he said, "you'd do nicely. Very nicely. It's rather a pity."

"I know," she said, and managed to sound sad. Two weeks, she thought, two weeks, two whole weeks — "We would have made such an attractive couple, too."

"But," he said, "think how red haired they all would have been. Perhaps it's just as well."

"All?" she said. "What do you mean, all?"

"Now," he said, "take Brady. Take the commander. Marries into the same family and — look at them. Rolling in the stuff."

"Well," she said, "not really rolling."

"I'd consider it rolling. Rolling is as rolling does."

"My uncle the admiral," Dorcas said, "married it. Not for it — at least I don't think so. My mother the admiral's sister —" She sobered suddenly. She thought of her parents, who had died almost together, as if by — almost as if by — some deep agreement that neither would live without the other.

He touched her hand again. He was quick to follow. The touch said, We quit playing now. The touch said, It wasn't much of a game — just a little game.

"It's all right," she said. "Doctors don't make fortunes. Not in small towns they don't, anyway. Small towns in Indiana."

"I wish," Alan Kelley said, "I'd known your father. I wish I'd known you when you were a very small girl, and remembered the teachers you remember. I wish I'd been in the seventh grade of the Horace Mann School when you were in the third grade."

"The Longfellow," she said. "And — you

wouldn't have come within blocks of me. You'd have said, 'Girls!' No — more like 'Gu–rrls!' With a growl in it."

He told her that she must have known very unpleasant little boys. He told her that he had been a very pleasant little boy, polite and considerate always. Especially to little girls who had red hair. He said, "Since you haven't got money, it's very fortunate you have red hair, isn't it?"

"I," she said, "am terribly sorry about the money, Alan."

"Well," he said, "when we get to be admirals, we'll have a limousine with an enlisted driver. We'll have a Navy house. We'll buy food at commissary rates. We'll buy drinks at half price at the officers' club."

"That's nice," Dorcas said. "Of course, we'll be about — about what? About a hundred?"

"Little faith," he said. "That's what you've got. Little faith as well as no money. Only red hair. Probably, since I'm so unusually polite and considerate, I'll be an admiral by the time I'm — oh, forty-five or fifty. A small admiral, of course. But an —" He stopped. "You know," he said, "you're very lovely. I love you very much."

"Even if I haven't —" she began, and caught herself and was, oddly and for an instant, ashamed that she had not quite made the turn with him, since they went hand in hand. (Although now their physical hands no longer touched.) Not the game at this instant; not any of their games. "I know you do," she said, quietly. Then, for seconds, they said nothing. Then he looked around the restaurant and, when their waiter saw him, scribbled in the air. . . .

It was a little after midnight when he stopped the Ford outside the Maples Inn in North Wellwood.

"Why," he said, "do they name so many inns after trees?"

"There really is a guest room," she said. "Not a very big guest room, but —"

He shook his head.

"Brady and Caroline are there."

"I," Alan Kelley said, "am a polite and considerate Navy lieutenant, steeped in tradition. I am also allergic to — chaperonage."

"I wish it were — next Saturday," she said.

"Yes," he said. "But — we'll never wish days away, will we? Even waiting days."

He kissed her. He moved very suddenly, very resolutely, out of the little car.

" 'Get thee to a nunnery,' " he said, and she slid across the seat, behind the wheel, moving as quickly, as determinedly, as had he.

"Yah!" Dorcas Cameron said, and drove away — drove, for a block or two, rather more rapidly than was really necessary because she so little wanted to drive away at all.

Caroline Wilkins wakened very gently and lay awake, not surprised at wakefulness, although she supposed it was still the middle of the night, feeling at first no urgency of any kind. She wakened and listened. She heard, from the other bed, his slow, deep sleep-breathing. The bed isn't empty, she thought. It isn't empty.

She lay quietly, so as not to waken Brady. He woke easily — she supposed always, but knew only that when they were together he wakened so. If she turned in bed he would waken. It sometimes seemed to her — although of course that was absurd — that if she thought "loud" thoughts, even that wakened him. She did not want to waken him now; she did not want things in any way other than, in this gentle moment, they were. She wanted only to listen to his slow breathing and know that — for these cradled moments — the other bed was not empty. She would not think — did not think — that the bed would be empty again so soon; that, by Monday night — do not count the hours until Monday night — she would not hear Brady's sleep-breathing, could turn all she pleased and disturb no one; could think any thoughts she chose, and waken no one.

Awaken no one, worry no one. She had managed the last for hours now — held the little worry in her own mind, willed it to diminish. And — it had diminished; so greatly diminished that not even Brady, who seemed (she sometimes thought) to live in her mind as immediately as in his own, had sensed the shadow there. The little shadow — the immaterial shadow. The shadow from the past, bringing back, with a sudden flicker of darkness, those months not to be counted, not to be remembered.

Yet, she had remembered. When the telephone had rung the afternoon before, only minutes after Dorcas had left her to go to the party, and she had hurried to it, thinking it Brady again and heard the other voice — she had remembered. Not wanting to remember; thinking it almost forgotten.

Not forgotten. It could not, of course, be that, nor was there any real reason it should be. But a thing relegated to the past, where it belonged — to the life of another girl; a silly girl who had thought herself wise, long ago in a place far away. A thing fenced away there, isolated; a small aggregate of ancient facts, moldering, no longer having color or poignancy. "Forget it," Brady told her patiently, tenderly; had told her often. "It hasn't anything to do with us." And, gradually, that had come to be accepted, to be true.

And it *was* true. Not even a remembered voice — not, surely, the fact that the voice *was* remembered — could change that truth. It had nothing to do with them; had never had.

Yet — she would have to tell Brady about it — now that telling him would no longer mar the perfection of first rejoining. Tell him the fact — the fact of a telephone call out of long ago; tell him (which would, in a sense, be harder) that the voice, long stilled to her ears and she had thought to her mind, had been, from its first (interrogatory) mention of her name, recognized, familiar.

"So what?" Brady would say, when she told him. "You remember a voice."

(But he would say that, brush it off like that, only to brush it from her mind, because he would know it a shadow on her mind.)

So what? indeed, she told herself, lying quietly in bed, listening to the quiet sleep-breathing of a loved man in the other bed. He would be right when she told him; right to dismiss it. And, she did not doubt, in his own mind he would dismiss it, since he had an ability to live *now,* in the immediate moment of living. An ability, she thought (her mind digressing) I had always believed more a woman's than a man's. But, it seems, an ability not mine.

She willed her mind steady, willed "loud" thoughts out of it. Send those months back to the — the segregation ward. Nothing — and surely not this trivial thing — can bring them into now. I made a mistake. Long ago I made a mistake. Everybody does, Brady says, and Brady is right. When one is nineteen and certain — so very certain, so pathetically certain — one is entitled to make mistakes. And the mistakes made then do not really corrode, really blemish. They only — leave a little smudge; a smudge that fades slowly, that time erases.

It is because I am still too young, she thought; young enough to want past and present alike perfect, the whole thing of one perfect piece. Well, things aren't that way, and now is fine — the now of my life perfect. It is only because of that, she thought, because moments can shine so, that I fear "shadows." It is the mind's wariness; the mind's instinctive knocking on wood.

I should go to sleep, she thought, and thought then of her father and thought, Thank you, father; thank you very much for what you did — for everything, for taking the quick (but quickly passing) fury of a child you loved, and not being swayed by it. And, most of all, for being right. I must write him tomorrow, Caroline thought; it's been two weeks since I wrote him.

Very softly, she reached out toward the watch on the table between the beds. She did not think she made any sound, and looked at the glowing dial and saw that it was a little after two, and Brady Wilkins said, "Carry? You all right?"

"I'm here," she said, very gently. "I'm fine, Brade. Go to sleep."

She did not herself return to sleep until once more she had heard the soft sleep-breathing from the bed beside her own.

"Very tall," Margo Craig said, and sipped breakfast coffee. "Very large altogether. But with the smallest possible voice."

"Oh," Paul Craig said. "Mrs. Belsen. The big house at the corner of Parley Street."

"We'll see her?" Margo said. She lighted a cigarette. She said, "Oh, I'm sorry, Paul," to a husband who could not stand cigarette smoke — anybody's — until he had entirely finished breakfast. She put the cigarette out.

"Probably," Craig said. "From time to time."

"And the cute little old ladies? The Misses Something?"

"Monroe," he said. "Cute, Margo?"

"Perhaps that isn't the word," she said. "Perhaps the word is 'quaint.' "

"I doubt we'll see a great deal of them," Craig said. He smiled, faintly. "They're not exactly contemporaries of mine, my dear."

She was quick to say of course not; to add, that she had not meant anything so absurd. She said that she was only trying to sort people out; that he must remember they were all new to her, and met in quick succession. "And," she added, "when I already had a headache coming on. I'm so sorry about that, Paul."

"Sorry?" he said. "Nobody chooses to have a headache, my dear."

"All the same," Margo said and now, since Craig had finished, was himself shaking a cigarette from a pack — was, indeed, holding the pack out to her — lighted a cigarette. "A new wife among old friends. And, she — conks out." She used the alien word with just enough hesitancy to show her appreciation of its foreignness.

He nodded. He understood — even her use of the slangy word.

"Probably," he said, "we'll run into — oh — the Thayers. Jas Knight. At the country club. Not the Misses Monroe, I imagine. Or

Mrs. Belsen, come to that. Although I've seen her lunching there."

"With a hat?" The query was innocent. He smiled.

"Quite probably," he said. "A difference in generations, Margo."

She hesitated a moment. She said, "Only that? Because — in most places — that is —"

"More sophisticated places," he said. "If we have to use that word. The wearing of summer hats — I don't mean sun hats —"

"We mean the same thing," she said. "Little — little round hats, with flowers."

"Yes," he said. "At country clubs. On beaches and the like. Not many any more. A difference in traditions, of course. Something one finds in places like North Wellwood. A matter of — standards." He ground his cigarette out. "Probably," he said, "I sound stuffy to you. I find a good deal to be said for certain — standards."

"Oh," she said. "Of course. It's only a matter of — what is the word, Paul?"

"Mores?"

"Of course," she said. "In Maryland — but I suppose the attitudes are much the same. Only the ways of showing them —" She let it trail off. "The cute little thing with red hair?"

"The — ? Oh — a Miss Cameron. Lives

at the old Adams place with another girl —
a Mrs. Wilkins. They rent the place. I believe
Miss Cameron has a position of some sort in
the city. Commutes. Mrs. Wilkins's husband
is in the Navy, I understand."

"She wasn't at the party," Margo said. "At
least — of course, I met so many people I'd
never met before —"

"She got there late," Paul Craig said.
"Drove up just as we were leaving. With two
men."

"Oh," Margo said. "The very good-looking
blonde? In a white pique dress? With the red
summer necklace — a Florida sort of necklace?
One of the men was tall and had black hair
and the other —"

Craig's long face showed rather more
amusement than was common to it. He said
he gathered she had noticed them. He said
that yes, the very good-looking blonde was
Mrs. Wilkins.

"Mrs. Wilkins," she repeated. "The Adams
place." She nodded her head briefly. "Just
getting them straightened out," she said.
"One more — the red-faced man, rather
stocky and —"

But she stopped because, as was evident
from his face, her husband was thinking of
something else — of, she gathered, something
rather unpleasant. He had not heard her

words, but now he seemed to hear her silence.

"I'm sorry," he said. "Speaking of Mrs. Wilkins reminded me — I've decided I'll have to let Joe Parks go, Margo. He's proved not to be — trustworthy."

She raised her eyebrows. "But hasn't he worked here for years and —"

"Yes," he said, before she finished. "I thought him quite reliable. It seems I was wrong." She waited. "Nothing to bother you with," he said. He stood up. "No use putting it off," he said, and walked out of the breakfast room. She heard the slight click as he pressed a button in the base of the intercommunicating telephone. "Mrs. Parks?" he said. "Have Joe come up to the house, please." He waited a moment. "Yes," he said. "At once, Mrs. Parks."

# IV

The magazine which Dorcas Cameron assisted — to, admittedly, a minimal degree — in editing was published weekly and carried news. (More precisely, she sometimes thought but did not often say, its personal preference as to the news, the preference being that of editors of much greater importance.) As a result, it was edited seven days a week; as a further result, its staff was "staggered." (Dorcas thought of it so, sometimes with feeling.) As a final, and to her immediate, result, she was off on Monday, the thirtieth of June. And would much have preferred not to be.

"Not *tomorrow*," she said, with some indignation, to Lieutenant Alan Kelley at a little after eleven o'clock on the night of Sunday, the twenty-ninth. "But I'm *off* tomorrow."

"Nevertheless," he said, letting her move far enough away to be looked at, "that's the way the Navy says it is. To obtain second endorsement, reading: 'Reported. Proceed in accordance with basic orders.'"

"Of all the silly things," she said. "You have to go into New York to have some officer —"

"Probably," he said, "a chief."

"Be still," she told him. "To have somebody write something on your orders that merely says you are to go on doing what you are already ordered to do."

"And," Alan told her, "that I reported. All in accordance with Navy regs., which are immutable. You must remember, Dorcas, that you are a mere civilian."

"But," she said, "I'm *off*."

There was the slight semblance of a wail in this. Alan responded suitably.

"All right," she said, when she was again able. "That's all very well. Very nice. Kiss and leave. That's what it comes to."

"I'll be back by mid-afternoon," he told her. "You can take me over to this country club of yours and we'll have a nice round of golf. Followed by a nice set of tennis. Followed by several nice long drinks on the terrace, among the restricted flies."

"We can't help that," Dorcas said, being momentarily distracted. "This is Northern Westchester. When in the afternoon?"

It depended on the trains. He got a timetable out of his pocket and they looked at it by the map light. They made it 3:31 — 3:31 at Brewster.

"I shall," Alan said, "expect to be met."

It left her with a useless day — most of

a useless day. A lovely day, with the sun doing everything the sun can do, but with a breeze to moderate its efforts. A day no good to anyone, until 3:31 at Brewster.

And — a day alone. She drove the three of them — Caroline and Brady and Alan (Alan in uniform, and good-looking in it. The rat!) to Brewster for the 7:28. Caroline went, she said, to shop. She went, Dorcas thought, to have a slow and uncomfortable hour and forty-five minutes longer with Brady Wilkins — an hour and forty-five minutes retrieved from empty hours. She would come back with Alan. She would go to the club with them? Perhaps. Which meant she would not.

A whole long morning, much of an afternoon, to twiddle thumbs in. Oh, she could wash stockings. She could wash underthings. (After she had done the breakfast dishes.) She could sweep the terrace; she could walk down and admire the neatness of the stone fence Joe Parks had repaired for them in early spring. (Even on rented property, a stone fence which is only a heap of rubble is unbearable.) She could make her bed. (And was tempted to lie in it.) She could dust the living room. She could —

She could, she decided at about noon, go down to "the place," the sheltered saucer of sunlight, and sun-bathe. If she could not bring

Alan money, she could be brown for him. He said he liked them brown.

She wore a white robe, and beach shoes; she carried, bulky and recalcitrant, a beach mattress under her arm. She went out through the back door and down the path, two hundred yards to "the place." Some birds spoke of her intrusion. She stretched the mattress out in the sun, and took the robe off and stretched herself out on the mattress and put protective pads over her eyes, and felt the warmth begin — felt, too, the gentle touch of the moving air on her body. As she lay quiet, the birds accepted her, no longer quarreled with her. A bluejay sat on a branch of one of the young trees which surrounded "the place" and looked at her. He put his head on one side, to see if from that view she had a different appearance.

I'm done on this side, Dorcas thought, sleepily. I must turn over. But it was several minutes more before she aroused herself enough to turn on the mattress and lie face down. She must, she thought sleepily, remember not to go to sleep. Even with the start she had, she could not take too much of it. Alan might like them brown; he would certainly not want them blistered. He —

She did doze, nevertheless — lying brown and naked in the sun, with the gently moving

71

air caressing her.

But then, very abruptly, the birds began to talk again — to chatter, chirp angrily. "Be quiet," she said. "There is sun enough for all of —"

But then she was awake. The birds had accepted her. Why, then —

She twisted, sat up on the mattress. Sat up and faced a man — a thin, small man with straggling white hair, and white stubble on a thin, contorted face. The man stood just within the shelter of the circling trees. The little shadows of stirring leaves danced on him. He stared at her. His staring eyes seemed unnaturally fixed.

She reached for the robe, closed fingers on it, pulled it around her. And then the man began to talk. He did not talk loudly. His voice was harsh, jagged. Yet he spoke in a monotone.

"Vile," he said. "Vile — vile. Shameless. You — all of you — flaunting your bodies. The shameless ones. The —" He went on — horribly he went on.

She tried to close her ears to what he said, as she clutched the robe around her body. But the ugly words — the vile words — slashed into her mind. It was almost as if the words — the unbelievable words — were whips on her body, tearing through the protection of the thin robe.

For seconds she could only sit there, clutch the robe around her, cower under the words — the violation of the words hurled at her. For those seconds it was as if all innocence, and all brightness, had been driven from the world, and everything in it made as ugly as the ugly words.

The man — an old, frail man she saw now — did not move toward her. And, as she recovered a little from the first shock of this awakening — this unbelievable awakening — she realized that the torrent of words was without real form; that, although the man did not raise his voice, he still shouted at her a denunciation which was essentially without meaning and — this came to her rather suddenly — not directed at her in any real sense, not at a person named Dorcas Cameron. The frail old man, the man with straggled white hair, was screaming (although still the harsh voice was a monotone) at some horrid thing which existed only in his mind. At — at *sin*. That was it. At the sin of — wantonness. But she was not wanton.

It came back, then, into perspective. It was not the laceration of all innocence, the dimming of the sun, although momentarily it had seemed both. She was a young woman sunbathing, as thousands did when the sun shone, in a secluded place — her own place of seclusion. And he — Why, he's only a crazy old man!

"Go away," Dorcas said, and spoke gently, and spoke — and so surprised herself — without fear. "Go away now."

The old man stopped speaking. His eyes seemed to change; seemed to become only the weak eyes of age.

"What did you say?" the man asked her, and the voice was only an old voice, and quavered a little.

"You must go away," she said. "You're not supposed to be here." He stood for a moment and looked at her, but now, she thought, he hardly saw her. "You've no right to be here," she said. "You must go away, now."

"No right," he said. "No right." He spoke as if he were learning new words. "You say I've got no right?"

"No," she said. "None. You're not supposed to be here."

For a second longer he looked at her, and then he shook his head a little, jerkily. And then he turned and went away — went through the trees and the brush beyond, moving slowly. He went down the overgrown slope toward the brook below; the brook which marked the limit of the land which belonged with the old Adams house. After a little time she could no longer see the man but could still hear the sound of his progress through the bushes. Then she could hear nothing.

She put the beach shoes on, then, and got into the robe she had held over her and rolled the mattress up — doing all these things quite methodically — and walked back up the path to the house.

What an awful thing, she thought; what an awful thing to happen. But already the shock was gone. The poor crazy old thing, she thought.

But all the same, she thought, after she had showered, dressed, I can't just forget it. He's harmless and he's — sick. But all the same, he shouldn't be wandering around. He should be taken care of, somehow. I ought to call —

I know, she thought. I'll go over and ask the professor what I ought to do. Perhaps the old man is known, known as harmless, tolerated. The professor will know. I can drive by and if he is sitting on the terrace, I can drive up and ask him what to do about the crazy — but certainly nasty — old man.

Walter Brinkley was sitting on the terrace. When she drove up he bounced out of his chair and bounced toward her, and smiled and said, "How nice. How very nice." But then he looked at her and said, "Is everything

75

all right, my dear?"

"Well —" she said.

He took her to the terrace; he said, "Harry?" and, when Harry appeared, "Bring Miss Cameron a drink."

Harry said, "Yassuh," at his broadest. He said, " 'Noon, ma'am," and went away.

She told Walter Brinkley. His round pink face sobered; he shook his head.

"Poor old Ash," he said. "Everybody thought he was all right again. I suppose —" But, then, he spoke reluctantly. "Can't have him bothering people," he said. "I suppose he was — very unpleasant?"

"Yes," she said. "Said — all sorts of things, Mr. Brinkley."

"But — didn't do anything? Threaten you?"

"I told him to go away," she said. "That he didn't belong there. And — he went away. Like a child."

"Yes," Brinkley said. "He does. There's no harm in him. Not that kind of harm, at any rate. Still —"

Again he hesitated. Then Harry Washington came out with a frosty glass and a frosty shaker and poured a daiquiri.

"Old Ash is having spells again, Harry," Brinkley said. "Showed up and — said unpleasant things to Miss Cameron."

"No," Harry said. "That's a shame, miss.

That's a real shame. He's got a screw loose, miss." He turned to Brinkley. "They'll lock him up again," he said.

He was no longer the old retainer; he was (Brinkley noticed) a man of the community, talking with another about a problem of the community.

"Yes," Brinkley said. "I suppose so."

Dorcas waited. He turned to her.

"A neighborhood problem," he said, and his smile invited her to join in solving it. "The man who — said unpleasant things — is Ashley Adams. In his late seventies. One of the family which owns the house you and your cousin are renting. A — I suppose one might say a lapsed member. Part of a lapsed branch. Been here since Revolutionary times, the Adamses have. Very much the usual story — a little inbreeding here and there, a bit of degeneration in spots. So — Old Ash has spells. They put him away from time to time — he's got a son who's a substantial enough citizen — Young Ash. He goes a long time between spells and they let him out again. The boy — I suppose Young Ash must be around fifty, Harry?"

"About that," Harry said.

"Takes care of him," Brinkley said. "For the most part, the old man merely putters around. Like any old man. Sits in the sun."

Professor Brinkley looked around his sunny terrace.

"Like any old man," he repeated. He was silent for a moment. "Now and then he wanders off," he said. "Turns up odd places and — says odd things. With — biblical overtones, often enough. I suppose —"

"Not very," Dorcas said. "Still — I suppose that was part of it. He did rather — call down vengeance."

"He's against sin," Brinkley told her. "Very much. And, when he's having a spell, finds much that is sinful. He's — never harmed anyone, my dear. And — the spells are usually quite brief. Often — usually, I understand — a quiet word or two, a reasonable word or two and — he's just a doddering old man again. Telling him he didn't belong there — that was just the right thing to say. Probably knew, more or less, where he was — on Adams land. And, that he didn't belong there. However — I suppose it's time to lock him up again, as Harry says."

But he looked at her and seemed to wait, and Harry, also, looked at her and waited. For a moment she was puzzled. Then she thought, Why, I'm being asked to — join. To be part of a community conspiracy to — to let an old man who only now and then has a screw loose stay free to sit in the sun.

"The poor old thing," she said. "Of course not."

"I could," Brinkley said, "pass the word along to Young Ash. I shall do that. Suggest he keep his eyes open. But if you'd rather —"

"No," she said. "I'm glad you told me, Mr. Brinkley."

"You're a nice child," Brinkley said. "Will you stay and have lunch with an old man? Sit in the sun with him? And have — what, Harry?"

"Crab-meat salad," Harry said. "And I've — I'se got biscuits ready to put in, professor." Brinkley waited, expectantly. "Suh," Harry added.

Alan did not like it, and said he did not like it. He said it on the clubhouse terrace, after two sets of tennis — she had taken three games in the second, which she privately regarded as a suspicious circumstance — over gins and tonic. He said that probably the professor knew what he was talking about; that the professor seemed to be the kind of man who would. He said that one should remember, however, that there was always a first time.

"People keep saying that," Dorcas told him. "In spite of the fact that there doesn't

79

have to be. Anyway — what could he do? He's so frail. With one hand tied behind my back —"

Alan still did not like it much. For one thing — "I don't like blokes staring at my girl. *Even* blokes in their eighties." He looked at her. "Admitting," he said, "the considerable temptation. And — I gather the things he said were very unpleasant."

"Yes," she said, and did not specify, and was not asked to. "And I said 'boo!' and he went away. Anyway, Caroline and I usually go to the place together."

"I must drop by some afternoon," Alan said. He made a face of some sort. "How," he said, "do you like my leer?"

"I had a cat who could leer better," she told him. "A black cat with white feet."

"Probably easier if you've got whiskers," Alan said. "Another set. Or what?"

"What," she said. "I'll drop you at the inn and you'll change and I'll go home and change, and then I'll pick you up at the inn. And don't try to get out of it."

"I look forward to years of not getting out of it," Alan said. "With the greatest anticipation."

"We'll have to leave her a car at the station," Dorcas said, as they walked under big trees toward the club parking lot. "I'll pick you

80

up and take you back, and we'll take both cars to Brewster and leave one and —"

"We must," he said, with gravity, "synchronize our watches. What if Carry hadn't caught you before you left?"

"There's usually a taxi," she said. "Or, she could have caught us at the club. But — she did catch me."

Caroline had "caught" her cousin, by telephone, just as Dorcas was leaving to drive to Brewster and the 3:31. She had caught her to say that she had run into Joan Francis and that she and Joan were going to have cocktails and dinner and go to the theater, because Teddy had got himself tied up and Joan had the tickets. And — was everything all right?

"Fine," Dorcas had said. "Have fun."

"Oh," Caroline had said, "a ball, darling. The ball of the lone females on the town."

No point then, and no time anyway, to report on the misadventures of lone females who sun-bathed in "the place." She must, of course, warn Caroline, but the morning would do. Caroline was not likely to go sun-bathing in the middle of the night, and it would certainly be that by the time she clunked to Brewster on the last train, which did wait for those who had gone to the theater — if they hurried — but made up for that by stopping everywhere. Quite possibly, Carry would decide to stay overnight in town, with Joan.

Dorcas dropped Alan at the Maples Inn; she drove home and showered again and changed again and drove back and got Alan. They stopped at the house and got the other car — the commuting Ford — and drove (Alan in the convertible; the Ford needed understanding) to Brewster and left the Ford for Caroline and drove back, beyond Ridgefield, to Fox Hill, which is an inn on a hill. They sat on the terrace with the sun behind them, the shade of the converted mansion covering them, and what seemed half Connecticut stretched out in front, the late sun on its many hills. And afterward they had dinner by a window which looked out on the same hills, and after that they drove on winding roads — and got a little lost, which did not matter because all roads lead back to other roads — and parked to make their plans.

It was one of those evenings without flaw, except that, finally, the convertible stopped in front of the Maples Inn and, after they had sat a moment, neither speaking, Alan Kelley said, "Well —" slowly, as if when the word ended time would end, and got out of the car. That was a flaw. Driving alone for the few miles from North Wellwood Center to Hayride Lane was a flaw, too.

The Ford was not in the garage. But that

meant only that Caroline had, as planned, gone to the theater and was catching the last train. Dorcas went to bed and thought, I'll stay awake a little while and remember, and went instantly to sleep. After an hour or so she was awakened — partly awakened — by a sound and called out sleepily and Caroline said, "Hi. Go back to sleep."

It was touch and go in the morning. It was always touch and go, but most that when she had not gone early to bed, as a commuter should. She had time to look into the "master" bedroom, now again masterless, and see her cousin sleeping; she had time for instant coffee. She was almost at the Brewster station when she realized she had not told Caroline about the old man.

The diesel was hooting up the way when she jammed the Ford into a parking crack providentially available. She ran through the station, to the platform and was there when the train was, and Alan Kelley (not in uniform this time) was there already, one of a crowd of commuters, all of whom looked somewhat dazed. "Cut it fine, don't you?" Alan said, and boosted. They found a seat together — Providence was working overtime this morning.

They parted at the Grand Central and met again at lunchtime, but had no time for lunch

— had time only to get to the Municipal Building and get a paper which granted Lieutenant Alan Kelley, USN, permission to marry Dorcas Cameron, spinster, after the due period of waiting and on completion of the required tests.

She would need to get off Saturday, even though it wasn't her day, she told them at the office, and told them why.

"As I keep telling you," the man she had told said to the man to whom he passed the word, "when they look like that it's just a waste of time breaking them in."

They kept her very busy that afternoon — as if, in advance, to compensate for Saturday; too busy, until rather late for Dorcas to recall, again, that she had not warned Caroline about the old man. It didn't really matter, she told herself. It was really trivial. Nevertheless, a little after four, she telephoned the house. There was no answer to the telephone's ringing.

Alan was at the gate of the 5:12 Pawling Local-Express. "You certainly do cut it fine," he told her, as they ran down the ramp to the train. But again — how very well indeed Providence was co-operating — they found a seat together. She told him it was all right about Saturday and he said, "The whole day? Not just a long lunch hour? What I call damned decent."

He was told that he would be off on a destroyer, and she as alone as Caroline, and that she was poor at thumb-twiddling. But that did not need restating; that was part of the plan.

"I suppose," she said, "that Brady *is* off again."

"Seems to be," Alan said. "At least, he's not at 90 Church. Dropped by after you scurried back to the office, to see if maybe he had time for a bite of lunch and — no Brady. General expression of blank surprise, to start with; general suggestion that there never had been a lieutenant commander of that name. Until I told them to come off it and showed my I.D. Then the oh-*that*-Commander-Wilkins treatment, as if they came by the gross, and that he was on assignment. Then made like clams."

"What *does* he do?"

Alan Kelley raised sandy eyebrows.

"My dear child," Alan said. "Learn your place. I'm a low-down deck officer, with whom the Navy shares none of its secrets. Nothing above sonar, at any rate. Brady is —" He stopped. "Moves in higher circles," he said.

"You *do* know."

"No," he said. "They sent him to M.I.T.

So, I suppose, he's concerned with superior hardware. Not for the likes of us."

"At least," she said, "I'll know where you are. Within reason. Poor Carry."

The diesel hooted, in its lachrymose fashion, at the town of Brewster. But a third of those in the coach already were on their feet, reaching for attaché cases, for Schrafft packages picked up in obedience to instructions. As the train nears Brewster, a white church steeple appears among trees. It is then time to get up and reach for cases, for packages; time to stand in the aisle, faced toward exit, and wait.

"We'll go by and I'll change," Dorcas said. "Then we'll go by and you'll change. Then, we'll decide what."

The commuting Ford, Alan thought, seemed much happier now it was going home. Hoped to get out of the sun, probably. He stopped it in tree shade on the driveway of the house on Hayride Lane. The convertible was in the garage ahead.

"Come in and make yourself a drink," Dorcas said. "I won't be a minute. Talk to Carry."

But Caroline was not on the terrace, nor in the living room or the kitchen.

"Carry?" Dorcas called, her voice lifted.

She was not answered. She tried again, calling more loudly.

"Funny," she said. "She's usually here

when I get home. With a drink ready, usually. I wonder — The car is here?"

"Yes," Alan said. "Gone for a walk?"

"I shouldn't —" Dorcas said, and did not finish. "I don't suppose —" He waited.

"She might have gone down to 'the place,' " Dorcas said. "The place we sun-bathe. Except — it's shady there by this time and —" She stood for a moment, irresolute. She said, then, "Wait," and ran up the stairs. He heard her call once from above, and heard her feet as she moved above him from room to room. Then she came down again. She shook her head.

*"Carry?"* she called again, louder than before.

"Of course," she said then, "she might have gone to the place and — fallen asleep. She didn't get in until all hours and —"

"That's probably it," Alan said.

"I'll go see," Dorcas said. "But — you'll wait?"

He nodded.

She went across the terrace to a path which led downslope. After she had gone a hundred yards or so, the path turned behind bushes and he could no longer see her. He waited —

Waited until she screamed. The scream was high, with terror in it and anguish. He ran, then; ran down the unfamiliar path.

She stood, her back to him, within a circle of slender trees. She clung to a young tree with either hand. He thought, as he ran toward her, that in any instant she might fall. She looked down at the ground.

He put his hands on her shoulders, and she was shaking. He circled her with his arms and looked beyond her, looked at what was on the ground.

She turned then. Her face was utterly without color, her lips were moving — a slash of moving red in the whiteness of her face.

Dorcas put her face against his chest, and shook in his arms. He looked down and his arms tightened around the girl.

Caroline Wilkins had been lying face down on a beach mattress when she was killed. Shotgun, Alan Kelley thought, and had, momentarily, to fight against the working of his throat.

She had been lying face down. The charge from the gun had taken her in the loins.

The charge had not had much space to spread. Buckshot fired from close in tears at a body, and does hideous things to it.

# V

Dead for some hours when examined — dead possibly as long as eight hours. But the body had lain for some time in the sun's heat, which made a difference. Say — some time in the early afternoon. Death as near instantaneous as made no difference. But Heimrich had seen that.

Captain M. L. Heimrich, Bureau of Criminal Investigation, New York State Police, nodded. He had seen that. With the doctor beside him, Heimrich walked back toward the house — walked some yards behind men who carried a covered stretcher. "Made damn sure," the doctor said. "Used both barrels. One would have been plenty."

Plenty, Heimrich agreed. Fired from just within the circle of young trees which rimmed a cup of sun. From about ten feet away, then. Into the body of a girl stretched peacefully in the sun. Asleep, quite possibly, or dozing. "Into" was something of a euphemism, considering what the buckshot had done. Rain had not fallen in more than a week, and the sun had beaten down. So, no footprints. Nothing, at any rate, to help. Somebody had gone

89

away from the place through bushes, and a thorn had torn at clothing and they had threads of an indeterminate color — grayish would have to do — and apparently of wool. Item for the lab. But, nothing to prove the threads had been torn from fabric that day, or any particular day. Probably since the last rain but —

Sergeant Forniss waited at the white house, the old Adams house. He waited on the terrace. When Heimrich came up with the doctor, Forniss lifted eyebrows. "Thanks, doctor," Heimrich said, and watched while the doctor crossed the turnaround to his car. "What you saw," Heimrich said to Forniss. "Some hours. Number not specified, naturally."

"Nope," Forniss said. "When was it ever? A Professor Somebody's showed up. To — do whatever he could, he said. Let him in. O.K.?"

"Yes," Heimrich said. "Professor Brinkley, probably. Short, round-faced man with white hair?"

Forniss nodded.

"The girl's taking it pretty hard," he said. "Nasty thing to come on. For anybody."

Heimrich nodded. He crossed the terrace and opened the screen of the french doors and went into the living room. It was cooler there, and still light enough. Walter Brinkley was there, and his round pink face was drawn, anxious. A young man — a sandy-haired man — was there. Of course — the young man toward whom a girl with deep red hair had moved so eagerly seventy-two — a little more than seventy-two — hours ago. And the girl. He had never, Heimrich thought, seen anyone so — quenched.

She sat on a sofa, and the sandy-haired young man sat beside her, and held one of her hands. But she did not seem conscious of this, or of anything. She looked ahead and down, but with eyes — Heimrich thought — which saw nothing. With quenched eyes. The two men looked at Heimrich; the girl at nothing. Then the younger man said, "You're Heimrich, they say. My name's Kelley. Alan Kelley." Then he waited. Then he said, "It couldn't have been an accident. Or, could it?"

"Both barrels were fired," Heimrich said. "From very close. It's hard to see how, Mr. Kelley."

Then Dorcas spoke. Her voice was dull, without expression. She said, "It was my fault. I — I should have done something." She covered her face with her hands. She said, "I didn't even warn her." They could hardly hear her words.

Heimrich looked at her.

91

"Not taken anybody's word," she said. "Not even — Mr. Brinkley's. I can't —" But then she stopped, as if it were not worth while to go on. Alan Kelley put an arm around her. She did not seem to feel the arm around her.

"Dorcas," Alan said. "Listen to me."

She did turn to him, then. She said, "I'm listening. But, it's true. What can you say when it's true?"

"That you did what seemed the right thing to do," he told her. "If it wasn't, it wasn't. But — that's all anybody can do, Dorcas."

"Not enough," she said. "Oh — I know all that. And I'm alive and Carry's — dead." Then she put her hands over her eyes, and her body began to shake. "I didn't tell her," she said.

"She thinks it was Ashley Adams," Brinkley said. "And — perhaps it was. I was the one told her not to worry. Persuaded her it wasn't important." He turned from Heimrich, who stood and looked down at them. Brinkley turned to the girl. He said, "Shall I tell the captain?"

"No," she said. "It was — what I did. Didn't do. All you could say was what you thought." She took her hands down from her face and now looked at Heimrich, and now saw him.

"Yesterday," she said. "I was down —

down there. Where she —" Her voice stopped; she drew in a breath which shook her slender body. "Was killed," Dorcas said. "A man — a man Mr. Brinkley thinks must have been this Ash Adams. He —"

She told him. When she had finished she said, "So, you see?"

"Yes," he said. "And, you may be right, Miss Cameron. I don't deny that. Only —"

For a moment he closed his eyes. She might well be right; it was even quite likely she was. And, if she was, that she might never forget — never really forget — what she might have done and had not done. A crazed man; a man frantically against "sin," intent on destroying "sin." And — a girl who sinned by lying naked in the sun. One day he might have gone away, but the next returned, this time with the weapon of destruction. And found, again, a girl lying naked in the sun — sinning in her nakedness.

"I still," Brinkley said, "can't believe it was Old Ash. He's — harmless. I'd have sworn he was harmless. In effect, I did. If there was a fault, it was mine. I've told her that. Tried to get her to understand that."

There might be enough faulting to go around, Heimrich thought, and merely nodded his head.

"When did it happen?" Alan Kelley asked

and, when Heimrich said that they could not be sure, but sometime around midday, Alan said, "Oh," in a flat tone. And the girl seemed to shiver and covered her face again with her hands. "We were both in New York," Kelley said, although nothing in Heimrich's attitude asked him about that.

"Her husband?" Heimrich said, and Alan Kelley shook his head slowly. He said that he had tried to get hold of Wilkins; said he had had no luck.

"Oh," he said, "they'll check. Call me back. But, I'm not sure that anybody — anybody locally — really knows. He worked — I guess he worked — on instructions from Washington. And, as far as I could tell, they think I'm an — unauthorized person."

Heimrich waited. Alan told him about Lieutenant Commander Brady Wilkins — what he knew about Wilkins's work, which was, in effect, nothing. Something he supposed, to do with "devices." Very secret devices. Involving, he supposed, high secret collaboration with suppliers. But what it came to, he didn't know anything about it. He doubted whether, in fact, much was known at 90 Church, even by the higher brass at 90 Church. Including, quite possibly, where, precisely, Commander Wilkins was at the moment. Or, had been since, Monday morning, he had parted from his wife, and from Alan Kelley, at Grand Central Station.

"I'll keep on trying," Alan said.

"Her parents?" Heimrich said.

Alan Kelley looked, momentarily, toward Dorcas. She did not look at him.

"We've got a call in for her father," Kelley said. "Her mother's dead — died several years ago, I think. The admiral — Caroline's father's a retired admiral — seems to be off somewhere in that cruiser of his. They're trying to get in touch. But, that's in California."

The girl, Heimrich thought, did not seem to hear any of this; seemed far under, far away. Heimrich did not like it, for the girl, for anybody. Not, he supposed, that Dorcas Cameron knew any more than she had told. Oh yes, one thing.

"This man, Miss Cameron," he said, and had to wait while his words seeped down to the girl's mind. "The man Mr. Brinkley thinks was Ashley Adams." He waited again. She lifted her head and looked at him. "How was he dressed?"

"I don't —" she said, but stopped. "Overalls?" she said, uncertainly. "Blue, I think. And — a sweater over a white shirt. With a collar button in the shirt and no collar."

"The color of the sweater?"

"No real color," she said and then, "Gray,

95

I think. A coat sweater."

Gray sweater, in spite of the warmth of the day. But blood moves sluggishly in old men. Gray sweater; gray thread raveled out by a thorn.

Ashley Adams was, obviously, the one to start with. Quite likely it would end with him, which would make it simple, if meaningless; which would make it bad for the girl. It was worst for her now, so soon after what she had seen. The shock would lessen, wear off. But — was even what she had seen quite enough to quench her as she seemed quenched? Even that and a sense of guilt? For action not taken, warning not given?

Apparently, Heimrich decided; and said that he would start with Adams, and that he hoped Commander Wilkins was found, and told. He said he would be back, and walked toward the terrace door. Walter Brinkley came after him. On the terrace, Heimrich stopped until Brinkley came up to him, but Brinkley took his arm and led him farther away, out onto the gravel of the turnaround.

"You think it was Ash Adams?" Brinkley said, then, and Heimrich said it seemed quite likely.

"I can't believe it," Brinkley said. "I suppose you're right, but — I still can't believe it. He's never hurt anyone. Never threatened to. Just, when he was having one of his spells, denounced people. He railed at me, once — on Main Street, in the Center. Came up and began to denounce me, in a rather strange, harsh voice — as if what he said were on a record —"

Walter Brinkley stopped himself. I'm wandering on again, he thought. Going into detail that doesn't mean anything.

"What I'm getting at," he said, "there was no threat. No suggestion of any threat. He'd got the idea I was a — a 'scoffer.' I don't know how, since I'm not." He paused; paused, Heimrich thought, for one of those inner examinations of words used, thoughts held, which were characteristic of Brinkley. "Or, don't think I am," Brinkley said, after the examination.

"No," Heimrich said, "I don't imagine you are. But — you could have been wrong about the old man."

"I hope not," Brinkley said. "I most earnestly hope not. For the girl's sake, chiefly." He moved his head toward the house to identify the girl. "I've made mistakes before; reached bad judgments before. They depress me but — there you are. With the girl —"

He paused, his round face very serious, very worried.

"She and young Kelley got a marriage

license today," he said. "He told me that, just before you came. She'd gone out of the room for a moment. Got it during her lunch hour, I gather. At — perhaps at — about the time Caroline was being killed. She — I'm afraid she blames herself for having been — happy. Coming home happy, with her boy and — finding what she found. I didn't see Caroline. Shirked that. But — it was pretty bad?"

"Yes," Heimrich said. "It was bad."

"A sensitive child," Brinkley said. "Coming on something like that, at a time like that. Even without this feeling of guilt." He looked at Heimrich. "Like shooting down a bird in flight," he said. "In flight, in song."

Heimrich nodded his head.

"I do hope," Brinkley said, "that it wasn't Ash Adams. For her sake. I do hope that, captain."

The house was square, white, with a front porch. A strip sign on top of the mailbox said, "A. Adams. Elect. Contr." It was one of a row of small, neat houses, each on a quarter acre of land, each facing the road which ran east from North Wellwood Center toward Connecticut. Sergeant Forniss stopped the car on the shoulder of the road in front of the house and he and Heimrich got out and started up the straight driveway which ran to a one-car garage beside the house. A man came out on the porch and waited for them.

He was a man, Heimrich thought, in his early fifties — a solid man, not tall, who wore slacks and a dark polo shirt, stretched tight over a swelling chest. When they were near enough, Heimrich said, "Mr. Adams?"

The man said, "Yep."

"State Police," Heimrich said. "Your father around?"

"Somewhere," Young Ash Adams said. "Maybe out back. Maybe out having a walk." He stared at Heimrich. "So," he said, "the professor changed his mind. Or was it the girl herself?"

"The girl?" Heimrich said.

"This Miss Cameron," Adams said. Unexpectedly, he spread his hands in a gesture of resignation. "All right," he said. "Can't blame her, I suppose. How's she to know? Poor, harmless old guy wouldn't hurt a fly. But how's she to know?"

"It's more —" Heimrich began but Young Ash Adams went on talking, and Heimrich let him talk.

"Just words, like always," he said. "I told the professor we'd keep an eye on him. Better eye on him. But — well, hell, I guess it's no good. Put him back in — in the loony bin. Only — he sure as hell likes to walk around.

The poor old —" He stopped, shrugged. "O.K." he said. "Back he goes."

"The professor told you about the — incident?"

"Uh-huh. Told the wife and she told me and I called him back. Thought he, and Miss Cameron, weren't going to — well, make a point of it. But — could be, they're right this way. Only — the poor old guy. All he does is sound off. Oh, I see the girl's point. I suppose he — called down vengeance?"

"Pretty much, I gather," Heimrich said. "But — I'm not here about that, Mr. Adams. About — something a lot worse, I'm afraid." He watched apprehension grow on Ash Adams's face. "Yes," Heimrich said. "Murder. Mrs. Wilkins, Miss Cameron's cousin. And — at the same place, Mr. Adams. Sunbathing at the same place. Early this afternoon."

Adams's face stiffened. He said, *"God!"*

Heimrich waited.

"I — I don't believe it," Adams said. "Not that it was the old man. I tell you —" But he gave it up with that.

"Where is he?" Heimrich asked.

"Like I said. Around —" Again he stopped. "O.K." he said. "I don't know exactly. Here when I left this morning. Sitting right here on the porch. The wife says he was here until eleven o'clock, maybe. Had something to eat and — went for a walk."

It was obvious. "You've checked up already," Heimrich said. "Had you heard already? About Mrs. Wilkins?"

"No," Adams said. "Only about Miss Cameron. That — well, that's all over town. I told some friends, asked them to keep an eye out for him. All the same, there was nothing this morning — or last night, come to that — to show he was having a spell. You can prove he was around there today?"

"No," Heimrich said. "Not yet, anyway. You got a shotgun, Mr. Adams?"

"So," Adams said, "that was it. Shotgun. Yep. Twelve-gauge. Got a patch of garden out back and there's a family of woodchucks —" He stopped.

"Let's have a look at the gun," Heimrich said.

Adams looked at him for a moment. Then, without saying anything, he went into the house. They could hear a woman's voice, but not the words. They could hear what Adams said — "State Police. That Mrs. Wilkins's been killed. They think the old man —"

"Oh Ash," the woman said. "I've kept telling you. Now — trouble. More —"

But she did not go on with that, obviously — Heimrich thought — because Ash Adams had walked away from her. They could hear his heavy steps inside the house. After a time he came out with a double-barreled shotgun — an old gun. A gun, Heimrich discovered quickly, which had been cleaned since it was last fired — barrels cleaned and wiped off; stock cleaned. With a rag which had a little oil on it.

"When did you clean it?" Heimrich asked.

"Hell," Adams said, "week ago. Had a go at the varmint. Missed him."

"You keep it locked up? Or could your father have taken it? Without your wife's noticing?"

"It's in a closet," Adams said. "Yes — I suppose he could. The wife's got things to do."

"Taken it," Heimrich said. "Brought it back. Cleaned it."

"He'd never hurt anybody," Adams said. "Never has. Never would. Ask up at Wingdale. They'll tell you that. Harmless. That's why, when he gets over a spell, they let him out."

That was why — that and the fact that the State hospital at Wingdale, like all such hospitals everywhere, had, always, more patients than it could handle; took the optimistic view, sometimes, in a kind of desperation.

"He'll have to be found," Heimrich said.

"Talked to. He — remembers what happens?"

"Mostly," Adams said. "But sometimes he gets a little fuzzy. Look, mister — you didn't say what your name was." Heimrich told him. "Look, captain — it wouldn't be murder."

"No," Heimrich said. "But the woman's dead, all the same. We'll take the gun along, Mr. Adams."

*"Ash!"* Ash Adams's wife called from inside the house.

"In a minute," Adams said. "It figures you'd want to take the gun. Listen — this makes it easy for you, don't it?"

"Now Mr. Adams," Heimrich said. "Like rolling off a log. Naturally." He spoke in a certain way.

"All right," Adams said. "Forget I said it. All the same. Could be somebody had it in for her. Or wanted something she had. Like money. Hear she's got a lot of money. Had a lot."

"Do you?" Heimrich said. "I don't know, Mr. Adams."

"Hired Joe Parks couple months ago," Adams said. "Had him straightening up an old stone fence. And they don't even own the place. Paid two dollars an hour. Won't get it back from high and mighty James."

Heimrich had turned to go down the porch steps. He turned back. It couldn't matter less, but he mildly wondered what Ash Adams was talking about. He said, "James?"

"James Adams," Ash said. "Same name as mine. Same family, you go back far enough. Owns the house they rented."

"Oh," Heimrich said, and started down again.

"Joe Parks lost his job account of working for them," Ash Adams said. "Regular job, that is. Job taking care of the Craig place. Seems old man Craig figured Parks was laying down on his real job and fired him. Seems he'd told Parks to pretty much stay on the property. Parks is sore as hell, from what I hear."

"At Mr. Craig?"

"Sure," Adams said. "But hell, he was always sore at Craig. At this Mrs. Wilkins. Calling her names at the tavern last night, fellow told me. Says she promised to keep it quiet he'd been working for her and figures she didn't."

"All right," Heimrich said. "When your father shows up, call the sub-station. A man will be over. Be sure you do that, Mr. Adams."

"O.K," Adams said, and turned around and went into the house.

Heimrich and Sergeant Forniss went back to the car. They used the radio telephone to start a search going for Ashley Adams, Senior.

"Parks," Forniss said. "Red herring, defense exhibit A."

"Naturally," Heimrich said. "Can't really blame him, though. Adams, I mean. And — I suppose we'll have to have one of the boys talk to Parks, Charlie."

"Yep," Charles Forniss said. "But what the hell. Suppose he did get fired for that. Makes Craig out an old meanie. But anybody could have known he was working for the girls. You don't point up a wall without somebody seeing you. Anybody could have told Craig."

"Yes," Heimrich said. "And — anybody could have used a shotgun. Any shotgun. Not like a rifle or a revolver. Anonymous little round balls. And — lots of people around here have shotguns, Charlie. Women who are alone nights, a good many times. Scare off marauders."

"Yep," Forniss said. "Miss Cameron and Mrs. Wilkins, you think?"

"We'll look around."

"You're not so sold on the old man?"

"Now Charlie," Heimrich said. "We have to shop around, don't we?"

Neighbors had rallied. Two young women, "ranch-house set" women, had rallied, one of them with phenobarbital. Dorcas Cameron was in bed. "You just leave her alone tonight," one of the young women said to Heimrich, and was a lithe young cat, defending. She stood, defiant, at the foot of the staircase leading to the upper floor.

Then Alan Kelley came down the stairs, walking carefully, making little noise. Heimrich started to speak and Kelley put a finger across his lips. Heimrich and Forniss went with him, across the living room, out onto the terrace.

"All right now," Kelley said. "She's finally got to sleep. Room's on the other side of the house and — you don't have to bother her any more tonight, do you?"

"I wanted —" Heimrich began.

"I got hold of the admiral," Kelley said. "That is, they got him on ship-to-shore phone. He was out on his cruiser. The Navy's flying him back. So far, I haven't been able to get in touch with Brady. And —" He hesitated. He shrugged.

"I was going to get in touch with you," he said. "The girls had a shotgun. Kept it in the hall closet. Being here alone —" He shrugged again.

"Naturally," Heimrich said. "Wise precaution. I suppose — you said 'had,' lieutenant?"

"Yes," Kelley said. "Anyway, it isn't there now. Could be somewhere else in the house, but Dorcas says they always kept it there. Kept it handy. So — it's gone."

They went back into the house, into the entrance hall. The door to the hall closet was a little open. Heimrich opened it further. The gun had, it was clear, been stood, butt down, on a felt mat. The butt had left an impress on the mat. Heimrich made sure the gun was not elsewhere in the closet. He closed the closet door. It did not stay fully closed.

"Warped," Kelley said, speaking low. "Lot of old houses —"

"I know," Heimrich said.

He moved back until he stood just inside the front door. Standing there, he could see into the partly opened closet. Dark in there, at the moment. But, in daylight, anyone standing at the door could have seen a shotgun in the closet. If, of course, there had been one there.

# VI

The sun wakened her. For moments, still only half wakened, she lay in a lovely floating between wakefulness and sleep. The first moments were ones of peace, assurance. She and Alan —

But then she saw that the sun was not in the right place — that the patch it made on the floor was too near the window, which meant that the sun had risen higher than it should have risen. It was like that on Sundays, not on days with a train to catch. The alarm clock must —

And then, before she remembered why, sadness came down on her like fog — sadness and a kind of desolation. She turned in bed and, for seconds, pressed her face in the pillow, shutting out light and the new day. But she could not shut out memory. Caroline was dead — dead through her fault, her indifference; her taking of the easier way. If I had stood by idly and watched her drown, thinking that somebody else would do something, somebody else save her, it would be the same, Dorcas Cameron thought. If I had known a bridge was out, and not warned her.

With that, although she buried her face in the pillow, pulled the pillow around her head with both hands, the picture of Caroline lying dead, lying torn, on a mattress soaked with blood, was hideously vivid in Dorcas's mind. The darkness she pulled around her could not dim the picture.

She lay so for seconds and thought, It's no good, this is no good, and turned to lie on her back and look up at nothing, lost still in a fog of sadness. But after a time that was no good, either, and she got out of bed and, slowly, making each movement a conscious thing — that might be the way — put clothes on — pants and bra and shoes and a yellow linen dress.

The house was silent, hushed. There had been people there the night before — Sally Blake (was it Sally?) and a girl who had come with her, and a square, solid man with a square solid face and very blue eyes. And Alan. And others — who had been there? I can't think, she thought. Something's happened to my mind — all numb, all dead.

She went downstairs slowly, going consciously down each step. She went into the living room, and then could hear that somebody was in the kitchen. She went out to the kitchen. Alan was pouring boiling water on coffee in a glass coffeemaker. Why was

Alan there? Why —

He put the kettle down and came to her and put his arms around her and she could feel his strong, wiry body pressing against hers. He held her so for a moment, without speaking, and then released her so that he could look into her face.

"It'll be all right," Alan said. He held her and looked at her. "Come back," he said.

She smiled — she could feel the smile on her lips so it must be that she smiled. She said, "I've not gone anywhere. It's only — oh, Alan, it's all so awful."

And with that, the fog diminished, the fog and the numbness of her mind. The sadness stayed; a kind of hopelessness stayed. But — he was real. And she was real and all of it.

"Good," he said. "Ought to be ready now," and turned to look at the coffee dripping through the filter paper. He spoke as if this were any morning in any life, and did not, yet, try to do more. Why, she thought, he must have stayed here all night. Slept on the big sofa. The coffee was hot and fragrant and afterward, because he expected her to, she ate an egg and a little toast. He drank coffee and watched her while she ate.

"Good," he said. "Now — snap out of it."

His tone, suddenly, was crisp. It was as if he spoke crisply to awaken her.

"I'll try," she said, and then, "I'll be all right, after awhile."

"You did what anybody would do," he said. "Get that into your mind. You asked a man who ought to have known and that was all you could do. However it turns out."

"I didn't warn her," she said. "Oh — I called once. Late — too late. She must have been dead then and —"

She broke. He held her close and she shook in his arms.

"Listen," he said. "Because you'd been convinced there wasn't really anything to warn her against. Not anything real. No — danger. You couldn't know he'd be able to get hold of a gun."

She sobbed still. He could only hold her. After a time she said, "I'm sorry. I'll try, Alan." And then, as she grew quieter in his arms, she said, "They're coming back?"

"The police? I don't know. I suppose they will. Your uncle's on his way. Gave him a very special ride, probably, so it won't be long. Dorcas —"

He paused. She stirred in his arms. He released her.

"I told him about the gun," he said.

"Of course," she said, and then the picture came again, and she put her hands over both eyes. But only for a moment. "We were here alone so often at night," she said. "Somebody — Brade, I think — said we ought to have a gun and — fire it into the air, if anybody bothered us. To frighten them away."

"Yes," Alan said. "Did you? Fire it into the air. Or — did Caroline?"

He named the dead girl carefully, hesitantly.

"Why," she said. "No. I never did. And — " She hesitated. That was no good, either. "Caroline never did that I know of. Not when I was here. I never even touched it."

"Anyone coming in the front door could have seen the gun," Kelley said. "Heimrich tried it. After they left I did myself. Would have been in plain sight, if anyone happened to look."

"Oh," she said. "They think — but how could he?"

"The old man?" he said. "I don't see how he could. Look, Dorcas. It doesn't have to be old Adams. You realize that, don't you?"

"Yes," she said. "But — he was awful, Alan. You didn't see him. What does he say? They must —"

"When Heimrich was here," Alan said, "they hadn't found him. Apparently he's — wandered off." He looked at her face. "That doesn't prove anything," he said.

"I know," she said. "It doesn't prove anything. But there's no use pretending —"

Knocking on the front door interrupted her. It was firm knocking, unhurried, without special demand.

They both went to the door, down the hall from the kitchen.

Captain Heimrich was the one who had knocked. He said, "Good morning, Miss Cameron. Lieutenant." He said, "All right, sergeant," but they had already seen Sergeant Forniss and a small old man — an old man with straggly white hair, white stubble on his old face; an old man wearing blue trousers and a white, collar-band shirt, with a collar button in it. And, an old gray coat sweater, although already the day was hot.

Dorcas shrank back against Alan Kelley for a moment. But then she straightened and stood alone.

"Yes," she said. "He — you found him? Does he —" She did not finish that.

"Came home around midnight, his son says," Heimrich told her. "They waited until this morning to call us. But — did keep an eye on him. No, Miss Cameron. He's not clear about things, he says. There's no doubt this is the man?"

"None," she said.

"Don't remember," Ash Adams said. "Keep telling people, I don't remember everything." He looked at Dorcas. "Don't remember you," he said. His voice was not the harsh voice which had forced ugly words on her, words under which she had cowered. His voice quavered. "Don't mean to harm nobody," he said. "Sometimes I can't remember things."

"Take him down and show him the place, Charlie," Heimrich said. "Maybe he'll remember then." Forniss took the old man off around the house. He was, Alan Kelley thought, gentle with him. They watched him go. "Come in, captain," Dorcas said, and they went back into the cool shadows of the living room.

"Mrs. Wilkins's husband?" Heimrich asked.

"Nothing," Alan said. "Her father's on his way."

"The gun in the hall closet," Heimrich said. "When did you see it last, Miss Cameron?"

She looked at him a moment. Then she shook her head, the soft hair swaying.

"I don't know," she said. "It — it had been there for months. You don't — anyway I don't — see things that are always there."

"No," Heimrich said. "You've looked for it, I suppose? In the house."

"Pretty thoroughly," Alan Kelley said for her. "I don't think you'll find it, captain."

"No," Heimrich said. "I don't think we'll

find it either. The closet door wasn't kept locked, obviously."

"Never," she said. "Captain — he — the old man — he could have started in and seen the gun and —" She put her hands over her eyes.

"Miss Cameron," Heimrich said, "you shouldn't feel — responsible. Even if it turns out to have been the old man. We've talked to the people at the hospital. They agree with Mr. Brinkley that he's harmless. Always has been. Has spells of excitement and — talks wildly. So, even if they're wrong, you shouldn't blame yourself."

"Because others were wrong too?" she said. "But — thank you, captain. I suppose you're right — about facts. Not about — about the way it feels. If I'd warned —"

She did not finish. It was as if she had slipped under water. Alan again put his arms around her but, this time, she freed herself almost at once. But she tried to smile at Alan Kelley. It was a smile from under water.

Heimrich gave her time. There was nothing to be gained by giving her too much — nothing for him, nothing for her.

"I suppose you don't keep the front door locked during the daytime? When you're here? Or — even when you're down sun-bathing?"

"No," she said. "Oh — sometimes we do. Did. When we remembered it. You think somebody —"

"Obviously, it's possible," Heimrich said. "Anybody could have come to the front door. Knocked. Or called through the screen. Come in, when nobody answered. Seen the shotgun if the hall closet door was partly open."

"Wait a minute," Alan Kelley said. "Then — it wouldn't have been the old man. Adams.

"The first time," Kelley said. "The time he said those things to Dorcas, he went away down toward the valley. Toward the brook. Away from the house. I'd think he'd come the same way, wouldn't you? Not from the front of the house."

Heimrich looked at him.

"I suppose it doesn't follow," Alan said. "No, I suppose you're right. But — one gets the idea of the way something happened. Makes up a kind of picture of the way it must have happened. Mine was — well, the old man wandering around, on paths through the woods. Coming on Dorcas at 'the place' and — that setting him off. The same thing yesterday, in a way. Oh, coming back, half knowing what he was doing, to see if she was there again. To — what? Punish sin? But, to come to the front door." He paused. He shrugged.

"The trouble is," Heimrich said, "we're

trying — you're trying, lieutenant — to clear up, make logical, something that's basically fuzzy. We don't know what goes on in a mind like the old man's, naturally. We can only guess."

"Tell me about your cousin, Miss Cameron," Heimrich said and, in answer to the look in Dorcas's face, "Everything you can think of. She and Commander Wilkins had been married for several years? You and she came here last fall?"

"Oh," Dorcas said. "That sort of thing. About three years. Yes. Her father is a vice admiral — my uncle, that is. She is —" The clear voice faltered momentarily. "Was," Dorcas said, "about twenty-six. She was born in Missouri. A place called Odessa. Her mother — Aunt Helen; not my real aunt, of course — was born there and the admiral was in China or somewhere — my Uncle Jon — Jonathan, really. Does this matter?"

"I don't know," Heimrich said. "Probably not, Miss Cameron. A great deal we find out has no bearing. But —"

"Her mother died six or seven years ago," Dorcas said. "She had a good deal of money. She left part of it — half, I think, to Caroline outright. The rest to Uncle Jon. Captain Heimrich — this *can't* mean anything if — if it was Ash Adams." She looked at him with her eyes suddenly alive. "You think it was — someone else?"

There was, Heimrich thought, a kind of hope in her voice. Which was understandable. He said only that it was too early to be sure of anything. He said he supposed that, now, Mrs. Wilkins's money would go to her husband.

She has a very expressive face, Heimrich thought, watching the girl — watching her expression change, as if the room had darkened, or her mind darkened; saw rejection, almost outrage, mirrored in her face.

"Not *Brade!*" she said. "How — what a horrible thought!"

"Now Miss Cameron," Heimrich said. "Try to — stand away from it. I know it's hard. I don't suggest anything against the commander. Tell me more about your cousin."

Caroline Bennett, before she became Caroline Wilkins, had lived in a good many places, as the children of Navy families do. When the Hitler war started the Bennetts had been in France; after Pearl Harbor, Helen Bennett and Caroline had gone back to Missouri and the admiral — a captain then — had gone to the Pacific; Caroline, after the war, had gone to Missouri University for, Dorcas thought, two years or so. "These are just things she told me," Dorcas said. "Things I picked up. Her family and mine lived in different places. A different kind of life. All this can't have anything to do with — with what happened."

"Probably not," Heimrich said, and was patient. One could not tell what might have to do with anything until one had found out much that could not. It was, he thought, one of the things most difficult to explain to laymen; one of those most obvious to a policeman. He did not try now to explain it again.

They heard somebody talking. Heimrich went out onto the terrace. Sergeant Forniss was coming up the slope, walking behind Ash Adams. The old man's lips were moving; he seemed to be talking to himself. Forniss shrugged broad shoulders.

"Drury," Heimrich said, and a trooper came around the house. "Take Mr. Adams back to the sub-station, will you?" Heimrich said. "Then — come back here."

"Come along, Mr. Adams," Drury said, and Ash Adams went along. He was mumbling to himself, the words not clear. Heimrich could see no expression in the old eyes.

"He was there, all right," Forniss said. "It's very difficult to get anything out of him, of course. Anything that makes sense. But — he was there."

"Both times?"

"Forniss didn't know. He had taken the old man down to the cup of sunlight and said, "Remember, Mr. Adams?" The man had mumbled words that had little meaning. But then he had said, "Naked," and then, much more loudly, "Naked and wanton." But then, just as Forniss thought seeing the place had set him off again, Ash Adams had become quiet and shaken his head and said he didn't remember. Then he had turned, suddenly, and started to walk away — down a path toward the brook at the bottom of the valley which here, between the ridges characteristic of the area, was almost a ravine.

"Moves fast when he wants to," Forniss said, and that he had had a little trouble catching the old man. The way back would, normally, have brought them through the sunny circle in the trees, but as they neared it, Old Adams had tried to break away — to wrench himself away. So Forniss had brought him back in a circle around the place.

"Doesn't help much," Heimrich said. "He was there, of course. We know that from Miss Cameron. But — the second time?"

"I don't know," Forniss said. "At a guess, yes, captain. He's — afraid of the place. And — it's hard to put a finger on. Going down, he wasn't. Coming back — up the slope — he was. All of a sudden and — at just about the distance from it the gun was fired from."

"Let's go down," Heimrich said, and they went down, and Forniss showed Heimrich what he meant. At a certain point Adams had — "well, call it shied," Forniss said.

Heimrich stood at the spot. He crouched a little, making himself more nearly the old man's height. A man would, he thought, have at that place — about that place — first seen a girl sun-bathing. From the same spot he might have fired both barrels of a shotgun into a slender, defenseless body.

"Or," he said, sharing the obvious with Sergeant Forniss, "seen the girl dead. A very ugly thing to see. Found anybody who heard the shots?"

"Nope," Forniss said. "The professor's nearest. But he was in the village, he says. He and Harry Washington. And — you know how people are in the country. Hear shots and say, 'Somebody shooting at woodchucks again.' Or crows, or whatever. Or — hear and don't realize they heard. The old man saw something. Or — did something. Got a shock."

Forniss was standing so that he faced toward the distant road. "Got visitors," he said. Heimrich turned. A black Volkswagen turned into the drive and began to trot up it. It trotted around the unmarked police car and settled down. A very tall young man got out of it, by stages. Standing beside the little car, looking over it, it seemed entirely improbable that he had ever been in it. He came across to the terrace and to Heimrich and Forniss, who waited. Even Sergeant Forniss had, by a few inches, to look up to the tall young man — tall and broad shouldered, with an unconcealing face and blond hair in a brush cut.

"This Commander Wilkins's place?" he said, in a pleasant, open voice.

Heimrich said it was.

"Man called from here," the tall young man said. "Identified himself as a naval officer. Name of Kelley, he said. Tried to find out where he could get in touch with Commander Wilkins."

He was very crisp. He was also, Heimrich thought, very authoritative.

"One of you?" the man said.

"No," Heimrich said. "And, who are you?"

"Right you are," the man said. "Don't blame you." He looked at the house, however, doubtfully. He looked, also with doubt, at Heimrich and Forniss. Although he was hatless, he gave, somehow, the impression of a man peering cautiously from under the pulled-down brim of a slouch hat.

"We're police officers," Heimrich said.

"Lieutenant Kelley did call from here, certainly. In an effort to find Commander Wilkins. In order to tell him that his wife has been murdered." He made a guess. "You're from the Navy?"

"May as well," the man said. He took a wallet from his pocket, held it out so that the I.D. card showed. He was, it appeared, Howard Nelson, Lieutenant, DV-S, USNR. He put the wallet back in his pocket.

"Like to see yours, if I may," Lieutenant Nelson said. "Matter of form."

Gravely, Heimrich showed his own identification. Lieutenant Nelson looked at it. He looked at Sergeant Forniss. He said, "If you don't mind?" Forniss, expressionless — only Heimrich suspected that, if Forniss's immobile face revealed anything, it would reveal amusement — proffered his own I.D. card. Lieutenant Nelson examined it with care. Then he leaned toward the two solid policemen. He spoke in a very low voice. He said, "Navy Intelligence." Then he stood back and looked at them with an expression Heimrich did not immediately fathom. Then it came to him. Lieutenant Nelson was looking at them keenly.

Heimrich felt that more was expected of him than he had available. He thought of saying, "Ah," in a certain way or even, possibly, "Ah-

*ha.*" He decided he was inadequate to either. The conspiratorial note would simply not be there. He did, however, refrain from saying, as he was somewhat tempted to say, "Think of that, now."

"I see, lieutenant," Captain Heimrich said. "I suppose — checking on the call? I can assure you it was quite what it purported to be."

"Um-m," Lieutenant Nelson said. "This naval officer. Kelley? What's his rank, by the way?"

"Same as yours," Heimrich said.

"Senior grade?"

"I believe so," Heimrich said. He watched the tall representative of Naval Intelligence make a mental note.

"He's around?" Nelson asked, the note made.

"Inside," Heimrich said and again was tempted and this time succumbed. "Regular Navy," Heimrich said. "Annapolis. Class ring."

Nelson said, "Oh." Then he said, "Of course." He turned toward the french doors.

"Wait," Heimrich said. "You are checking up? Or — have you come to tell us where we can get in touch with Commander Wilkins?"

Nelson turned back. He looked doubtful.

"Lieutenant," Heimrich said, and there was no longer any amusement in his voice, or in his mind. "Mrs. Wilkins has been very brutally murdered. We haven't yet been able to inform her husband. Do you know where he is?"

"The issue," Nelson said, "is security, captain."

"The issue," Heimrich said, "is a man's wife dead and a man not told. Do you know where he is?"

"Well," Nelson said. "Personally, I don't. But —"

He stopped. Again he looked at Captain Heimrich and again looked keenly, as if from under a lowered hat brim.

"A man calls up to enquire about an officer," he said. "An officer whose whereabouts aren't supposed to be a matter of common knowledge. This man who calls *says* he's a naval officer. Says he's a friend of this other officer."

"Kelley called," Heimrich said. "To ask how to get in touch with Wilkins. Let's keep it simple. Your point, naturally, how did they know the man who called was Lieutenant Kelley? Did it ever occur to them to look up Commander Wilkins's telephone number and call back?"

"All right," Nelson said. "We do that. A

man answers. Says he is Lieutenant Kelley. All we know is, he's at Commander Wilkins's house. What does that prove?"

"You know," Forniss said, "he's got something there, captain. Yep. He's got something there."

He had, of course. Heimrich tries to be a fair man. He nodded his head.

"All right," he said. "You satisfy yourself that Lieutenant Kelley is Lieutenant Kelley. That there is reason to get in touch with the commander. Then what? You drive back to New York, identify yourself, whisper to somebody that Kelley is Kelley?"

Nelson looked, Heimrich thought, a little hurt. I am, Heimrich thought, being unfair to the serious boy. He thought, in fact, that Nelson flushed just perceptibly.

"Telephone," he said. "And — identify myself by a code number. All right with you, captain?"

"Quite all right," Heimrich said. "Lieutenant Kelley's inside someplace. Satisfy yourself and make your call."

The tall man went in. Through the open doors they heard him say, "Lieutenant Kelley?" After a time, they heard him use the telephone. He said, "Nelson here" and then something in so low a tone that they could not hear it. (He had, Heimrich deduced, to

126

repeat it in a tone not quite so secure.) He said, "Seems to be Lieutenant Kelley. And — the commander's wife's been killed." Then he listened. After some little time, he came out again to the terrace.

"They'll get in touch with him," Lieutenant Nelson said. "He'll be here in an hour or so. 'Copter to Danbury."

"Oh," Heimrich said. "I gather he's not far away, then."

"Not far," Nelson admitted.

"Good," Heimrich said. "I thought he might be in a rocket to the moon."

"Did you?" Nelson said. "No, captain. And, by the way, I'm instructed to stay on for a while. Lend a hand."

"Oh," Captain M. L. Heimrich said.

# VII

Walter Brinkley was deeply disturbed, which was to be expected — a woman (who should have had life before her) had been shot to death half a mile, if that, from the desk he sat at; another girl agonizingly thought herself to blame and, in fact, if blame there were it was as much his as hers. (More — infinitely more.) The innocence of a place, a community, he loved had been most brutally mutilated; the tranquility shattered. He felt both outrage and persisting shock. And, strive as he would, he could not keep his mind from imagining the girl dead, and the details of the shattering wound. (Since he was a man unfamiliar with violence, his imagined picture was by no means adequate. It was quite bad enough.)

But, since a scholar must learn to toughen his mind against even the sharper facets of the outside world, and since Brinkley was a scholar, this deep disquiet, sadness, might not have stopped his work. It was, nevertheless, stopped. He had been discussing the persistence in American English of certain verbal forms abandoned in England — "gotten," for example. From this theme, in itself fascinating, his mind insisted on slipping away.

Brinkley took his hands from the typewriter keys at around eleven o'clock that Wednesday morning and lighted a cigarette. He leaned back in his desk chair and looked out the window he faced. He could look along the ridge and make out the Adams house and part of the driveway. There were several cars on the driveway now. He supposed that one of them belonged to his friend Heimrich. (He had begun to think of Heimrich as a friend.)

What made it impossible for him to concentrate was, Walter Brinkley decided, not, basically, the murder itself, deeply as that affected him. It was some aspect, some detail, that distracted him, pricked exasperatingly at his mind. An aspect of the whole — the quite dreadful whole. But, Walter Brinkley thought, some aspect which concerns me — me especially. It was, he thought, like a speck on the lens of an eyeglass, irritatingly present, yet subconsciously rather than consciously apprehended. (Until finally one removed glasses, polished lenses.)

Brinkley removed his own, abstractedly, and polished them, but it was not, of course, anything so simple as that. As nearly as he could decide, what it was was something he had either forgotten, or improperly understood. It had to do with the murder of Caroline Wilkins. He was sure of that. But, with somebody else too, and who the somebody else was he could not for the life of him remember. Then the Misses Monroe came into his mind. It was as if the Misses Monroe were part of it. Nothing could be more absurd, obviously.

Of course, he had encountered the Misses Monroe, and their aged chauffeur, the day before at the A. & P. in the village. Miss Elvina — or perhaps it was Miss Martha — was pinching heads of lettuce. Brinkley himself had stopped in to get a loaf of french bread. Afterward, he had stood briefly on the sidewalk in front of the A. & P. and chatted with the Misses Monroe while the chauffeur, aided by a clerk, had carried their purchases out to the Rolls. He remembered Miss Martha — or perhaps Miss Elvina — had said that they tried to buy for as much of a week as possible and the other sister — Miss Elvina almost surely — had said that they had never been able to bring themselves just to call up Gristedes, although they knew many people did, because they wanted to *see* things.

It could hardly have been that which now was a burr in his mind. Had something else, something pertinent, been said? He could think of nothing.

Yet vaguely — most vaguely — Walter

Brinkley felt that the burr *had* been set then, the pricking started then or, actually, a little later. *Wait* — it must have been at about the time he talked on the sunny sidewalk with the Misses Monroe that Caroline Wilkins was killed. Could it be as simple as that?

He considered. He tried to think that it was as simple as that. He failed. There was something else, and he could not go on with his work until he had got — he did not himself employ the form "gotten" — to the bottom of it. It was not, of course, certain, or even entirely probable, that when he got to the bottom he would find the Misses Monroe there. Looked at soberly, it seemed most improbable. Tentatively, he rejected the Misses Monroe, and waited for something else to appear on the mind's radar. Nothing did. All that appeared was, again, the two little old ladies and a sunny stretch of sidewalk in front of the A. & P. Miss Elvina had, sometime in the course of their chat, mentioned how convenient their Deepfreeze had turned out to be, although they had hesitated so long to invest in it. Not that, certainly.

In such, or similar, circumstances, the police tried to recreate past events. At least, he had heard they did, or read they did. But he could hardly ask the Misses Monroe to meet him, again, on the sidewalk in front of the

A. & P. and talk, briefly, about food purchases and the advantages of food freezers. The Misses Monroe, although not especially censorious, might well think that a little odd of him. Poor old Walter, they might think, how eccentric he's becoming. How like a professor.

But he might, he thought, invite them to lunch at the Maples. That in itself would be rather odd, since it was unprecedented, and since he had seen them the day before and in fact, three days before that. And not previously in a month or more. If only he could think of a good excuse. He tried to. The only thing that occurred to him was that he might ask advice on the purchase of a home freezer but that he almost at once rejected as preposterous. The Misses Monroe were not, to put it as mildly as possible, people one asked about mechanical devices. Nonetheless, the bottom had to be got to. Momentarily, he wondered whether Harry might not have a solution. But he asked too much of Harry.

How I fuss over things, Walter Brinkley reflected, and became a man of action. He looked up the telephone number of "Monroe, Misses, the," and dialed it and, when answered, said, "Elvina?"

It was Martha. But she did as well, being — or was that really Elvina? — a year or two the older and hence the one to make decisions.

"Why Walter!" Miss Martha said, on being asked. "How *nice*. We'd love to." She did not even seem particularly surprised. I waste too much time mulling things over, Walter Brinkley thought, after he had replaced the telephone. Probably it is better to do things first and wonder why afterward, like other people. He went downstairs, where Harry was polishing silver (it being Wednesday) and said that he was taking the Misses Monroe to the Maples Inn for lunch.

"You are?" Harry said, too startled to say "You is?" He made up for it. "Yas *suh!*" he said, which was going rather far even for Harry Washington. Worriedly, Walter Brinkley hoped that his taking the Misses Monroe out to lunch, instead of having them here to lunch, would not hurt Harry's feelings. Harry took pride in his cooking, and his pride was justified. "You have so much to do on Wednesdays," Brinkley said.

"Yes suh," Harry said, and then, "Are the police making any progress?", speaking as one resident of North Wellwood to another, about the thing uppermost in all minds.

"I don't know," Brinkley said. "Unless — we turn out to be wrong about Old Ash."

"I'll be surprised," Harry said. "Very surprised. So will everybody." By the last he meant, and Brinkley knew he meant, all those of North Wellwood with whom Professor Brinkley, and others of pinkish skin, would not have social contact — except, of course, at the annual dinner of the N.A.A.C.P. The "everybody" of Harry Washington's term knew, Brinkley suspected, a good deal more about North Wellwood than he himself did. Their reported opinion was reassuring.

"A little psychotic," Harry said, of Ash Adams. "Senile dementia, probably. But harmless. You wants I should drive you, professor, suh?" (Protean was the word for Harry; a word, anyway.)

"No need," Brinkley said and when, at a little after noon — the appointment was for twelve-thirty, but the Misses Monroe would almost certainly be early — Brinkley left for the village, he drove himself, in an M.G., which he drove rather rapidly and with something like professional competence.

The Maples Inn had a parlor — a parlor every inch a parlor. The Misses Monroe were waiting in it. They wore silk dresses and little hats with flowers and each wore a glove on her left hand and carried the other glove in it.

"So *nice* of you, Walter," Miss Elvina said and Miss Martha said, "So *very* nice." Whereupon, Walter Brinkley was conscious of some inward embarrassment, almost guilt, since he had an ulterior motive, if only he could think what it was. And the sweet old things —

"A sherry," Miss Martha said, at the table in the dining room, on being pressed. "A very small sherry." She had taken off both white gloves, and placed them in her lap. So had Miss Elvina. "A sherry would be *very* nice," Miss Elvina said. "But you must have whatever you usually have," Miss Martha said. "We know how men are," Miss Elvina said, achieving, Walter Brinkley thought briefly, perhaps the greatest exaggeration of recent times.

The sherries came. Brinkley's martini came.

"We understand," Miss Martha said, holding her glass delicately (but without, of course, extended fingers), sipping from it gently, "we understand that she was quite — unclothed."

"Oh dear," Miss Elvina said. "We *did* hear that, Walter."

Walter Brinkley had supposed they would come to it quickly; he supposed that, throughout North Wellwood, people were coming to it quickly. He had not, however, supposed that they would come from precisely that direction. He realized at once, however, that any other direction of approach would hardly have occurred to the Misses Monroe. First things first, of course.

"Well," Brinkley said, "she was sun-bathing. In a secluded place. On her own land."

"The Adams land, really," Miss Martha said. "But it does come to the same thing, I suppose. So tragic."

Brinkley was momentarily distracted by the word "tragic," which he feels should be used to describe only events great in dimension. He pulled himself back.

"So difficult," Miss Elvina said, "so *very* difficult, isn't it, to think of such a thing occurring in North Wellwood? Mrs. Lambert says that, already, the inn has had several requests for reservations. From *reporters*."

"Well," Brinkley said — how often, in chatting with the Misses Monroe, he found himself beginning sentences with "well!" — "such things happen in many places, Elvina. I suppose we can't hope to be excluded."

"But," Miss Martha said, "in North *Well*wood, Walter."

"But you know, dear," Miss Elvina said, "there was poor Mr. Woodbridge."

Mr. Woodbridge, Walter Brinkley remembered after a moment, had recently hanged himself in his garage. Miss Martha was not, however, taken aback.

"The poor man," she said. "But — not really North Wellwood. Not really. He had an apartment in New York, you know, dear."

If this was to come to anything, was to ease the nagging in his mind, it would, Brinkley decided, have to be guided. The difficulty was, of course, that he did not know in what direction.

"As for that," he said, "Mrs. Wilkins had lived here only a short time. She and her cousin, the poor child. She's very upset, you know."

"We must," Miss Martha said to Miss Elvina, "send flowers. That is — I suppose —" The pink tissue of her still-pretty face crinkled in thought. "I suppose one does?" This was to Brinkley, who found himself puzzled, also. Flowers to a house of death, certainly. But, did that cover murder? It was a point he had not previously had cause to consider.

"Well," he said. "Perhaps when funeral arrangements have been —" He let it drift away. "The cousin," he said. "Dorcas Cameron. A very sweet child. She was sun-bathing in the same place Monday and it seems that Old Ash Adams — spied on her. And, said unpleasant things."

"We did hear that," Miss Martha said. "Who was it told us, dear? And that Miss Cameron blames herself for not reporting him to the authorities. But I'm sure poor Ash would not harm anyone."

"So was I," Brinkley said. "I told her that. We may be wrong about him, I'm afraid."

"Ash?" Miss Elvina said, with obvious surprise. "Only an absent-minded elderly man. One grows a little that way as one grows older, I'm afraid. But — the Adamses are a very fine old Wellwood family, Walter."

"Well," Brinkley said, "perhaps a little more than absent-minded, Elvina. But, it is difficult to imagine anything of this kind. I agree to that."

"Someone from outside," Miss Martha said. "Oh, the special, I think." The last was to the waiter. "Yes," Miss Elvina said. "The special, please."

The special was chicken blinis, and it was very good. And Mrs. Lambert, who operated the inn, had once told Walter Brinkley that, when she looked out the window and saw the garden club ladies coming, she sent word at once to the kitchen to put the blinis on. "Lamb chops, please," Brinkley said, "and — perhaps another sherry?" The last was to the Misses Monroe, who looked at each other. "So delicious," Miss Martha said. "A very small one." "So delicious," Miss Elvina said. "Two sherries and a martini," Walter Brinkley said. "From outside, Martha?"

"I'd think so," Miss Martha said, and Miss Elvina nodded her head, associating herself.

"So many new people. From so many places, really. It's all quite changed since our father's day. Coming down from Brewster in a carriage. It took rather a long time, of course."

"From so many places," Miss Elvina said. "Chicago and places like that. I understand that Mrs. Wilkins and her cousin are from the Middle West. Not that it matters at all, I suppose."

"We mustn't be provincial, dear," Miss Martha said. "Whatever will Walter think? But of course, it is true. The old Farmer place — out on the Ridgefield Road, you know — the people living there now are French. Actually, Walter. Something to do with perfumes, I understand."

"Well," Brinkley said — how sadly often, indeed, he was using the soft wedge of the word "well" — "well, President Roosevelt once started a speech before the D.A.R. with 'fellow immigrants.' " He immediately wished he had said something else.

"Dear Walter," Miss Martha said, her tone making allowances. "Very amusing, I'm sure. But — wasn't it in rather doubtful taste? Particularly since the Roosevelts are, after all, quite an old family."

Which had, Brinkley thought, been rather the cream of the jest, and so intended. But this time he did not say what he thought. He said, "We must expect change, of course," which seemed safe enough. Sherries arrived, and a martini. A man with a camera swinging around his neck looked into the dining room. What he saw appeared to fill him with morose thoughts. He withdrew, probably toward the taproom. The press, Walter Brinkley decided.

"— from Maryland," Miss Elvina was saying when his thoughts returned. "She'll find the climate rather difficult, I'm afraid. Do you remember poor Mr. Bingham, dear? And the ice storm? Mr. Bingham was from Louisiana, Walter."

"I," Miss Martha said, "have always found our climate very bracing. Quite probably Mrs. Craig will also. She seems quite nice. Younger than Paul, of course. But I'm sure she'll fit in perfectly."

It was none of this, obviously; this was getting him to the bottom of nothing. Almost certainly, his impression that the nagging had started after he talked on the sidewalk to the Misses Monroe was without value. Walter Brinkley continued with his martini. Then he thought of something.

"All the same," he said, for once avoiding "well," "ice storms can be very unpleasant. With the power failing and that sort of thing. The freezer stopping."

At least, they had talked about a Deepfreeze

in front of the A. & P. Not, so far as he could recall, about anybody who had come from Louisiana.

"We thought of that," Miss Martha said. "And — you know what we did, Walter? We had a generator installed. To make electricity, you know."

"Although," Miss Elvina said, "at our ages —"

Buying groceries to last a week. A home freezer. What else had they talked about in front of the A. & P.? They finished drinks. The waiter returned with chicken blinis and lamb chops. They tasted.

"Delicious," Miss Martha said. "Mrs. Lambert has such a good chef."

His cocktail party?

"They made the canapés Saturday," Brinkley said. "Did rather well by us, I thought."

"Such a lovely party," Miss Elvina said, making Walter Brinkley feel as if he had been fishing. "So many interesting people. So nice to see —"

If he had been fishing, as he supposed he had, Walter Brinkley found his net filled, since the Misses Monroe remembered the party with much pleasure and in very considerable detail. Walter Brinkley listened carefully, thinking that this might well be it. He listened through lunch, and through coffee after it, and until he saw the Misses Monroe — "So sweet of you to have us, Walter." "Such a really *friendly* thought" — into their ancient Rolls and got himself into his M.G. Then he examined the net.

The result was depressing. If there had been anything in the net, it had got out through the mesh. That's what my mind is, Walter Brinkley thought. My mind's a mesh.

# VIII

There had been reporters; a good many reporters. "It's up to you, naturally," Heimrich had told her, but then, had added that it would, probably, be better if she got it over with. It had taken time to get it over with, since the reporters were difficult to satisfy and the photographers, it had seemed, would never be satisfied at all. Alan had been with her — Alan frowning, his eyes cold. It had been he who, finally, said that enough was enough. They had made her memories come back, since they were skilled at that, and wanted that. She had lived again — and for a moment had swayed, standing beside Alan — through the discovery of Caroline's stricken body. She had said that, yes, the old man, Ash Adams, had said things — dreadful things — when he stood on the edge of a circle of sunlight and stared at her.

"You thought he was a psychopath?" one of the reporters had asked and she had nodded and said, "Yes. I guess so," and then quickly, before she was asked, "Really I thought he was just a — a strange old man. Everybody seemed so —" But she stopped without finishing.

"Just one more," a photographer said. "Put your arm around her, lieutenant."

"You," Alan Kelley said, "can go to hell."

"Naughty," the photographer said, and took a picture of Alan Kelley glaring at him. He said, "Just a job, lieutenant."

"Far as I can make out," one of the reporters said, "nobody seems to know just where her husband was when it happened. That right, Miss Cameron?"

"He was —" she said.

Lieutenant Howard Nelson lent a hand then, as he had promised.

"Commander Wilkins was carrying out his duties," Lieutenant Nelson said, in a firm voice.

"Think of that now," one of the reporters said. "Just think of that. What duties?" Lieutenant Nelson looked hurt.

It had gone on for some time; it had not, she realized, gone especially well. But there was no way, now, for anything to go well. And, in time, it had ended and the reporters had gone away, and the photographers. And Lieutenant Nelson had looked at his watch and left the terrace — where it had all been going on, because that was the way the photographers wanted it — and gone inside and used the telephone. He had come back and said, "Just took off from Chicago. Had to fuel up," and was speaking of the airplane which was bringing Admiral Jonathan Bennett to the place where his daughter had been killed. Then he had said he would be seeing them, to which neither Dorcas nor Alan said anything, and got into his Volkswagen and hopped away in it.

Then for an hour — almost an hour — things seemed to stop. They sat on the terrace in the shade of a big ash tree, and everything stopped, and her mind stopped. It was as if a film, transparent yet impenetrable, were between her and the stopped world — the sunlight on the grass seemed dimmed, as her mind was dimmed. Alan looked at her and there was worry in his eyes, and he seemed close and yet incredibly far away.

"You ought to eat something," he said once, and the prosaic words came from a great distance and she said, first, "What?" and then, without waiting for him to say the words again, "No, I don't want anything."

Then, after a time, she said, "I did mean to tell her. But everybody said he was just a harmless old —" And she did not finish, because it was not worth while finishing, and because there was the film between her and everything, even Alan.

He said something. This time she really

did not hear at first.

"Other people," he said, "knew about this place you sunbathed in?"

"Oh," she said, "I don't know. Does it make any —"

"Dorcas," he said. "Wake up, Dorcas."

"I suppose so," she said. "I don't know."

"Did you tell anybody?"

"I don't know," she said. "Who?"

He repeated it. "Anybody." He waited a moment. He said, "Listen, Dorcas," and she said, "I'm listening."

"I don't think it was the old man," Alan Kelley said. "Listen to me. I don't think Heimrich does. I think somebody came into the house and took the gun and — found her. At the place."

"Why?" she said. "What had Carry done to anybody?"

The reporters had been over that, and now they came full circle. Had Caroline Wilkins had any enemies? Anybody who hated her? Had threatened her? And, of course, she had had none. Heimrich had, at some time — sometime before he went off with the sergeant — asked the same thing, but as if it were only a formality to ask; almost as if he were reading a question from an established list of questions. Nobody had hated Caroline Wilkins. She had been sunny and gay and a good many had loved her, and none hated.

"That's it," Dorcas said now. "Don't you see that's it? That we have to admit that's it? She wasn't shot as — as a person. As Carry. Just as — as a sinful thing. Don't you see?"

"No," Alan said. "I don't see. And, you don't see. Had you mentioned this place? The place where you sun-bathed? Think, Dorcas."

"I don't —" she began, and then she did remember. It was trivial; it would have no meaning. Because the old man she should have warned against —

"Go on," he said. "You've remembered something."

Somebody at Professor Brinkley's party had said something about her tan; said it was a wonderful tan for so early in June; asked if she had brought it back from Florida or somewhere. And she had said — she remembered now having said — that she and Carry had found a wonderful place to sun in, and had got a very early start and had said, "A place down back of the house. Secluded. With trees around it like a screen." And she thought, too, that she had said they called it "the place."

He leaned toward her. And now, it seemed, the film had thinned; it seemed now that she might reach through it.

"Who were you talking to?" he asked her. She tried, her mind no longer numbed, to remember. But, in the end, she had to shake her head. She could not even guess.

"I didn't really know any of the people," she said. "Except the professor. And, after a while, the two little old ladies. The rest were — blurs. You know how it is."

"One person? Or a group of people?"

"Several, probably," she said. "There were most of the time little groups of people."

"That you and Carry both used the place?"

"Oh yes. I must have."

"Did you tell Heimrich about this?"

But then the film returned, and she shook her head slowly, tiredly. Because when she thought of telling Heimrich that she had mentioned "the place" at the party the fact that she had mentioned it seemed suddenly meaningless. He wanted real things; he wanted facts. This was — a wisp of vapor.

"I will," Alan said, and she said, "All right," from a long way off.

"When he gets back," Alan said. "I'll —"

The bell of a telephone, ringing inside the house, interrupted him. He said he'd get it and Dorcas nodded her head, dully. He went in. After a time he came out. "Professor Brinkley," he said. "Thought of something he wants to tell Heimrich. Doubts if it's of any importance but —" He ended with a shrug, the approximation of Walter

Brinkley's hanging doubt.

He went over and stood behind Dorcas and put a hand on each of her slender shoulders. She moved her head so that, for a moment, her cheek rested against his wrist. "I'll be all right," she said, and he said of course she would, but looked down at her and frowned. It was taking her a long time to come out of it, to be "all right."

Investigation of crime can be likened to a good many things and one of them (Captain Heimrich sometimes thinks) is the search carried on in turned garden soil for something lost there — a ring, for example. One looks with eyes and probes with fingers, but this is often not enough. The best way then is, patiently, perhaps more than once, to fill a sieve and shake it, also patiently, until what is of no importance has sifted out. Some tedium is involved, but in the end one is likely to find what is sought.

There are, of course, quicker ways to get the result desired, and these are employed by all policemen when they are available. The quickest, of course, is to have somebody approach, in the ordinary run of such things, by stealth, and say, in effect, "P-sst! There it is. Don't say I told you." But a stool pigeon does not often come to hand in private crime.

There is also the method of inspiration, which is fine if one happens to be inspired. It is Heimrich's gloomy belief that he seldom is. A study of character is likewise important, but that is part of the sifting. It is also useful, at times, to prod the animals into motion, which is frequently revealing. But that comes only when one knows which animals to prod. By that time one is usually looking more for proof than for identification.

While Lieutenant Alan Kelley waited to tell Captain Heimrich that anybody at the party might have known something — enough — of the cup of sunlight in which Caroline Wilkins had died, while Walter Brinkley, professor emeritus, waited to report something he supposed would be of no importance, Heimrich and Sergeant Forniss sifted. Others — everybody who could be rounded up, could be spared — helped.

A trooper in plain clothes drove up to Wingdale to talk to doctors — talk slowly and carefully, trying to forget nothing, miss nothing, about the mental condition of an old man named Ash Adams, who saw sin in nakedness. Another went — had gone the night before — to drink a good deal of beer in a rather run-down tavern and ask questions and listen to answers. His over-all impression was that a man named Joe Parks had really shot his mouth off on Saturday night when, it is true, a good many men do.

The matter of sifting Parks out might well, of course, be left to Sergeant Forniss, who was capable of discharging much more exacting tasks. Heimrich went himself, taking Forniss, for the simplest of reasons — he could not, at around noon on Wednesday, think of anything else specifically useful to do. Vice Admiral Bennett was somewhere in the air, and, with him, much information — most of which would have no value, but all of which had to be put into the sieve — about the past brief life of a dead girl. Lieutenant Commander Brady Wilkins was — if Lieutenant Harold Nelson knew what he was talking about — also somewhere in the air, bringing what he knew — and bringing, Heimrich supposed, bitter sorrow and helpless rage.

"Taking Wilkins quite a while," Forniss said as he drove the police car toward, and then along, Craig Lane. "Mostly when they use a 'copter it's for short hops. Our cloak and dagger boy did say 'copter,"

This was not a question. It was a reminder. It was something to say.

"Yes, Charlie," Heimrich, said. "It is taking quite a while."

"A convenient setup, in a way," Forniss said. "You've noticed that? Having where you were so secret that if you tell inquisitive cops the roof falls in. Imperiling national defense."

"Yes, Charlie," Heimrich, said. "I've noticed that, naturally."

"And," Forniss said, "she had the money. Goes to him, now. Biggest chunk of it, anyway. They haven't got hold of her lawyer yet?"

Caroline Wilkins's lawyer had offices in New York. He would know if she had drawn up a will. He was, however, in court. His return was being awaited.

"Not yet, Charlie," Heimrich said. "Here it is."

Forniss started to turn into the driveway where a mailbox marked, austerely, "Craig" did sentry duty. He had to slow, then stop, to let a battered Ford, driven by a dark-haired man, come out. Heimrich glanced at the man, hoping he was not Joe Parks. From the description he had got of Joe Parks this man wasn't. Younger by a lot.

Forniss did not start the car immediately. They both looked across lawns at the house.

"Why?" Heimrich said.

"God knows," Forniss said. "Mad architect, maybe?"

"Or," Heimrich said, "none at all. Somebody with a dream and a pile of shingles."

The gatehouse was just off the road, at the

right of the driveway. Furniture stood on the porch; it was evident the Parkses were moving out and hadn't yet. Forniss stopped the car in front of the gatehouse — brown-shingled, like the main house — and at once a small, gnarled man came out of it and stood and glared at them.

The man was in his sixties, at a guess. His hands were thick and twisted. He had heavy gray eyebrows and not much hair. He said, "Got no time to talk to anybody."

He fitted the description.

"Now Mr. Parks," Heimrich said. "It won't take long. What's this thing about your threatening Mrs. Wilkins? At the tavern the other night?"

"Lies," Parks said. "G.D. lies. Bunch of G.D. liars. All I said was, she got the old bastard to fire me. After ten–twelve years. Make something out of that?"

"Perhaps," Heimrich said. "Mrs. Wilkins is dead. You've got a shotgun?"

"Damn right," Parks said. "Got it right handy."

"Parks," Heimrich said. "We're the police. You talk a lot about what a woman has coming to her. She's found dead a day or so later."

He got out of the car. Forniss got out on the other side. They are both big men, with square and formidable faces. They stood fac-

153

ing the angry small man and looked down at him. He seemed to get smaller. Anger seemed to seep out of him.

"Man like me," he said, "gets no breaks. I didn't kill nobody." He paused. "Mister," he added.

They waited.

"So," he said, "I shot off my mouth. Had a couple. What's that supposed to mean?"

"I don't know," Heimrich said. "Tell me, Parks."

"Not a G.D. thing," Parks said. "I work for the old bastard ten–twelve years. This Miz Wilkins has me square up an old fence. Says she won't say nothing about it, on account the old bastard thinks he owns me. Even when he's off gallivanting on a yacht. Or whatever. Think I was a slave or something."

It took some ten minutes. Parks was not direct. That, with anger drained away, he turned querulous, did not help. Boiled down: Caroline Wilkins had told the old bastard (Paul Craig) that Parks had done a little work for her. Craig — from whom nothing better was to be expected — had fired Parks on the ground, apparently, of dereliction of duty. "Did everything there was to do and he can't say different." Parks had been incensed; after a few drinks, he had shot off his mouth about Mrs. Wilkins and — at somewhat lesser

154

length, since his hearers could be assumed to know what a bastard the old bastard was — about Craig. A long way from that to killing anybody.

"Which it is," Heimrich said, as they drove on up the drive, toward the monstrous house, with Parks glaring after them, regaining anger, shouting, "That's right! Don't take my word for nothing. Ask the bosses."

"One way to look at it, though," Forniss said, "is that damn near anything is a long way from being worth killing for. If you're sane. I notice you want Craig's version."

"Now Charlie," Heimrich said. "Since we're here."

The driveway was long. The police car took it at a comfortable pace. In the turnaround in front of the big house a Cadillac was parked, and a big Chrysler. As Forniss stopped the police car at a modest distance, a slender young woman in walking shorts, a young woman with black hair in tight curls on a head proudly held, stood up from a chair on the terrace and took off sun glasses to look at them. Then, across the several feet which separated her from the car she said, in a young, beautifully clear voice, "I'm sorry. We don't want anything."

That was unexpected, but only a little. It is almost the first thing people who live in country houses say to strange men in unimposing cars. Heimrich got out of the car and smiled at Margo Craig who said, "Oh, I'm so sorry," and smiled too, and walked across grass toward him.

"There was a man about storm windows," she said. "And then, just now, a man with brushes. I am sorry, Captain — Heimrich, isn't it?"

"Yes," Heimrich said. And he wondered if, for a moment, he could see Mr. Craig.

She hesitated. She said, "Well." She said, "The trouble is, captain, that Paul's having a conference. With Mr. Knight and some others. About the new high school some of the — well, Mr. Knight calls them johnny-come-latelies — are trying to get built. Of course, if it's really important? About this — this awful thing?"

"Not particularly important," Heimrich said. "Parks was heard to — say certain things. About Mrs. Wilkins. Under the circumstances, rather unfortunate things."

Her expressive face changed. It showed regret. She said, "The poor man. Poor Joe."

Margo Craig shook her head, regretting the plight of Joe Parks. She said, half to herself, "The poor old thing," and then, to Heimrich, to Forniss, "Won't both of you come and sit down? Perhaps, if you tell me what you want

156

to know? Only, of course, I don't really know much about Parks, except what my husband has told me." She paused. She smiled faintly. "Actually," she said, "I'm a johnny-come-lately too, you know."

They sat on the pleasant terrace. What they wanted to know was, what kind of a man was Joe Parks. Probably it was not important. It was one of the things which, having come up, must be disposed of.

Again, she only knew what her husband had told her. Parks had worked for Craig for years; he and his wife had acted as custodians for the big house, as caretakers, during Craig's many long periods of absence. Paul Craig had relied on Parks.

"A big place like this," Margo said, and something in her tone recognized, certainly did not apologize for, the rather absurd bigness of the place — "a big place like this has to be looked after. Paul trusted Parks. Even —"

She paused. She said, "I'm really only repeating what my husband told me, after he had to let Parks go." Heimrich nodded. "Well," she said, "Parks is — getting along. And, I'm afraid, getting so that he likes to drink a little more than he should. Paul made allowance but —" She paused again. "We have to have a reliable man," she said. "Someone who can really be trusted. Paul decided that Parks couldn't be and — had to let him go."

"Because," Heimrich said, "he — went absent without leave? To point up a stone wall for Mrs. Wilkins?"

She supposed so. At least, that that was the immediate thing — the last of many things. That he had done that and, when asked, denied it. "My husband," she said, "can't stand being lied to. He never lies himself and —" She raised and lowered delicate shoulders.

"Mrs. Wilkins did tell your husband Parks had worked for her?"

"Oh," she said, "I shouldn't think so. That seems rather absurd. I don't know that Paul even met Mrs. Wilkins before —" She stopped again. There was shock, now, in her expressive face. "Awful," she said. "Such a terrible, hideous thing!" She paused once again. "But," she said, "apparently poor Parks thought she had. I suppose, actually, that somebody saw him working on the wall and happened to mention it."

"Has Parks a bad temper?"

She shook her head at that. She said that, on her few times of meeting him, he had seemed merely polite — almost too polite, perhaps. But she knew, really, very little about him. If it was important, she supposed she could interrupt her husband and —

But then several men came through the french doors, onto the terrace. "Show these new people —" one of them, a short and red-faced man said, in a red-faced way, as they came out. He did not finish. He looked at Heimrich and Forniss somewhat balefully, for no reason Heimrich could think of — except that he probably was a baleful man.

There were three other men — two of them (and one of these Craig) tall and lean and, in expression, austere. The man who was not Craig, in particular, appeared to look at the world with disapproval. Certainly, disapproval was in the brief attention he gave to Heimrich and Forniss. The fourth man was younger, and he was large and affable and he nodded pleasantly to Heimrich, as if he knew him or were, at the least, quite ready to know him.

"Want me?" Craig said and Heimrich nodded. "In a moment," Craig said and then, "We'll work on it, Jerry," to the red-faced man who said, explosively, that there was damn little time. The three who, Heimrich gathered, stood with Paul Craig against modern fripperies — such as new high schools — went out to the large cars and away in them. And, being asked, about Parks, Craig hesitated a moment.

"You mean," he said, "because of the things

he's reported to have said about Mrs. Wilkins? Threats, I gather?"

"Yes," Heimrich said.

"He blusters," Craig said. "I doubt if it would go beyond that. Of course — " He let that hang. "For your information," he said, "Mrs. Wilkins did not tell me that Parks had worked for her. It was hardly a thing she would have thought it worth while to bring up."

"No," Heimrich said. "It was because he did some work for Mrs. Wilkins that you decided to let him go?"

"I employed him," Craig said, and now the austerity in his manner was somewhat more extreme. "I expect complete loyalty from those I employ."

"Naturally," Heimrich said. "He neglected his work?"

"Certainly," Craig said. "And, in any case, there was a matter of principle involved. A matter of integrity." He spoke somewhat as if he explained the obvious to the backward.

Once more, asked once more, he said that he did not think there was real violence, but only bluster, in Joe Parks. They thanked him and drove away from the remarkable house — and, Heimrich thought, the somewhat remarkable man.

"He," Forniss said, "should have lived a

hundred years ago."

"Yes," Heimrich said. "And, in a way, he does."

"Toe the line or walk the plank," Forniss said. "Done that sort of thing before, apparently. Tough on Parks. No wonder Mrs. Craig talks so careful-like." They drove for some time in silence. "Parks started off tough enough," Forniss said, then, "Came off it, though."

"We're cops," Heimrich said. "Fairly large ones, Charlie. Might make a difference, naturally. A woman, lying face down, defenseless — there'd be a difference."

Forniss, uncharacteristically, looked momentarily from the road toward Heimrich.

"No, Charlie," Heimrich said. "I'd be rather surprised."

"The old man?"

Heimrich shrugged. The old man had been there; the old man was, sometimes at least, irresponsible; when his mind reeled, the old man was an instrument against sin. How far the mind reeled, nobody — not psychiatrists or anybody — could do more than guess. The old man was obvious; the old man was opaque. The old man was easy, and murder is often easy. But — the old man did not really make it easy. You could come back to him only after you had been everywhere else, and then it would be a guess, and it would be a guess still if Ash Adams came to them and said, "Yes, I killed the naked girl," because that might well be, again, only fantasy in a troubled mind.

They stopped to telephone. Item: Caroline Wilkins's attorney had returned from court. She had made a will. All of which she died possessed went to her husband, Brady Wilkins. Item: The doctors at the state hospital at Wingdale were agreed that Ashley Adams had never shown violent tendencies. Efforts to entice them further onto limbs failed, as was to be expected. Item: A man who said his name was Peel wanted to get in touch with Heimrich, in regard to the Wilkins case.

"Why?" Heimrich asked.

Peel had not said. He had had a bad telephone connection with the police barracks in Hawthorne, and had hung up before the line could be cleared. He had, however, said he would try again.

Heimrich would be at the Wilkins place. If Peel called back, Peel could be told. "No first name?"

Presumably, but the first name had been a blur. That was the connection. "A crank?"

They could not help him there. Probably, of course, a crank — the less stable members of the public become very helpful in the investigation of crime, particularly a crime in which a young woman dies while lying naked in the sun. There would, particularly if a solution was not reached quickly, be more of them — many more of them, on telephone; offering counsel through the mails. The chances were a hundred to one, a thousand to one, that none of the counsel would be of value. The hundredth chance remained, the thousandth chance. So — Peel was to be told where Heimrich could be reached.

# IX

The big black car was stenciled "USN." It wore Navy license plates. It edged past the police car in the driveway and stopped in the turnaround. A sailor in the most immaculate of white hats, the most tailored of dress blues, got nimbly from behind the wheel and went around the car and opened the door for Vice Admiral Jonathan Bennett, retired. Jonathan Bennett got out, while the sailor stood at attention.

He looks so exactly like an admiral, Dorcas Cameron thought, and got up from a chair on the terrace. How can I ever face him, she thought, and faced him and began to walk toward him.

Bennett wore gray tweeds; he was lean and had a long brown face and stood erect, unbending. He did, certainly, look exactly like an admiral. He must have looked like that, Dorcas thought — vaguely, putting off other thoughts — almost since he was an ensign. Was that one reason he had, in fact, become an admiral? She supposed not; the Navy has admirals of all shapes and sizes, including some who are pudgy. Dorcas walked to the edge of the terrace and then Alan Kelley took two long steps and stood beside her, straight as the admiral stood.

Admiral Bennett walked across the grass and stopped and looked down at Dorcas. For the first time, she thought, there was age in Uncle Jon's face. She looked up at him, and did not know what was in her own face.

"All right, child," Bennett said, and smiled. (Except that it was not really a smile, only the shape of a smile.) "Not your fault."

Her lips trembled. She wanted to hide her face in her hands, but did not.

"It — it was," she said. "Uncle Jon — it —"

"That's not true, sir," Kelley said, and then he put an arm around Dorcas's shoulders and held her against him.

"Shouldn't suppose so," Bennett said. "Who are you?"

"Kelley, sir," Alan said. "Lieutenant."

Vice Admiral Bennett looked at him; looked at him carefully; looked at his hands. The ring was there.

"Get you a drink, sir?" Alan Kelley said.

"Yes," Bennett said. "And her, Kelley." Kelley went.

"Well?" Bennett said. "What did you mean, Dorcas?"

He went up onto the terrace and stood and

looked down at her.

"A crazy man," she said. "They said he was harmless. But — I should have done something. I — Uncle Jon, I'm so —" But she stopped. There did not seem to be a word for it.

"Goes without saying," Bennett told her, but his voice was a dead voice. "This man kill Carry?"

"They don't know," she said. "He — they think he was there. At the place where —"

"All right," Bennett said. "They told me enough. About that. What about the crazy man?"

She told him. She had half told him when Alan came back through the french doors, with a tray and glasses on it, and bottles. Just beyond the doors he stopped. Bennett did not look at him, but he stopped. Dorcas finished; she told it briefly.

"Sentimental fools," Bennett said. "Should keep him locked up. All right, Kelley."

Alan set the tray down on a table. "Scotch," Admiral Bennett said. "Whatever she wants. Have one yourself."

"Yes sir," Alan said, and poured.

"All right," Bennett said. "The point is, who's in charge? And, why isn't he here?"

"A man named Heimrich," Alan Kelley said. "Sir. I don't know where he is, at the moment. He seems to be a very efficient man, admiral."

"We'll see," Admiral Bennett said. He took his drink. He said, "Sit down, my dear. Drink your drink." When Dorcas sat down, he sat too. He said, "Sit down, Kelley." Alan sat down. Bennett looked over the top of his glass; looked, Alan Kelley thought, at nothing, through blank eyes. Or — did he look over water, endless water, and see ships battered down? He had, Alan Kelley knew; and seen men die — friends die. Alan wanted to say something, but there was nothing to say.

Bennett looked at him, then. He said, "All right, Kelley. Carry on."

The words had no precise meaning. But, surprised a little, Alan thought they were an answer to his thoughts.

"And you, child," Bennett said, and his voice was different — not so old, not so flat. "Told you to drink your drink. Apparently there's no proof this man who yelled at you had anything to do with — the rest of it. Not your fault, anyway." He looked at her, gray eyes intent. "That's an order," he said, and smiled, and this time the smile was a little more than a shape.

She sipped the drink. Poor Uncle Jon, she thought. On a boat in bright waters and a telephone rings and — this. She held the glass in her hands — both hands — and looked at it, and did not see it. She saw a circle of grass and horror there. Would she never see anything else? Really see anything else? Even — even Alan?

"My dear," Admiral Bennett said, "I won't have this. No fault of yours." His eyes made her look at him. "None," he said. "However it was." Then, abruptly, he looked at the watch on his wrist.

"Kelley," he said, "find out where this Heimrich is. Tell him to get along here. Tell him I want to see him."

Alan Kelley put his glass down and stood up, more or less at attention, as one does for admirals. But he said, a little hesitantly, "I don't know, sir. I —"

Admiral Bennett looked at him and Alan Kelley stopped.

"Yes sir," Kelley said and turned to go into the house. He took two steps.

"Kelley," Admiral Bennett said, and Alan stopped and turned back. "I'd appreciate it if you'd try to get in touch with this Heimrich," Bennett said. "And — thanks for standing by."

And again, as he went into the house to the telephone — supposing he had better try the police barracks first — it seemed to Alan Kelley that the vice admiral, retired, had answered thoughts unspoken. Quite an admiral this admiral must have been, Alan Kelley thought and then, unexpectedly, thought of Heimrich — not as a man to find, but as a man of square solidity and — He considered a word, and nodded and dialed Operator and waited. Yes, the word was right. A man with the habit of command.

It was, he thought, going to be interesting when the two — well, this word probably was "collided."

"I want —" he began, but then heard a car stop outside and looked through the front door. "Never mind," he said.

Captain Heimrich was getting out of the police car. He was not quite as tall as Admiral Bennett. On the other hand, he was a little thicker. It's a hell of a time to be amused, even on the surface of the mind, Alan Kelley thought, and went out onto the terrace to attend a collision.

The police car, with Forniss in it, backed and turned and went down the drive.

Heimrich walked across the grass to the terrace. He noted that Vice Admiral Jonathan Bennett, standing, waiting, looked very like an admiral should; he noted that the Navy had provided superior transportation, and that rank — even retired rank — retains its privileges. He noted that he was being regarded, assayed, through very level gray eyes.

"You're the man in charge?" Admiral Bennett said. It was not really a question.

"This is Admiral Bennett, Captain Heimrich," Alan Kelley said, at much the same time, and Bennett looked at him briefly and Alan stiffened somewhat.

"I'm very sorry about your daughter, admiral," Heimrich said, which was inadequate, as anything would be. For an instant, the gray eyes went blank, shuttering the tall man alone with pain which was nobody's business but his own. The blankness passed.

"Very well," Bennett said. "What have you to report, Heimrich?"

Heimrich closed his own eyes momentarily. He opened them.

"Now admiral," Heimrich said. "Nothing conclusive at the moment. We —"

"My daughter," Admiral Bennett said, "was killed more than twenty-four hours ago. Considerably more. If your reports are accurate."

"Yes," Heimrich said. "It's been less than that since Miss Cameron found the body." He managed to speak without inflection.

"Well?" Admiral Bennett said. "What action are you taking, Heimrich?"

Heimrich walked up onto the terrace, which was raised a foot or so above the lawn. Height was equalized, or nearly. If Admiral Bennett planned to be difficult, there was no point in looking up at him.

"What I think necessary, admiral," Heimrich said, still without inflection. "I appreciate how you must be feeling but —"

"That," Bennett said, "has nothing to do with it. Leave that out of it. I asked what progress you've made."

"And," Heimrich said, "I told you, nothing conclusive." Bennett looked at him, measured him.

"You *are* in charge?" Bennett said.

It seemed a good time.

"Yes," Heimrich said. "The responsibility is mine." He regarded Bennett, blue eyes as frosty as gray eyes. "Naturally," Heimrich said.

It was, as Alan Kelley had anticipated, collision, none the less direct for being, in the moment of its greatest intensity, silent — a matter of eyes only, of wills only. Alan found himself wondering whether anything precisely like it had happened to Admiral Bennett before, and thought it improbable. The admiral's life had been — as mine will be, Alan thought — so arranged that direct collision is unlikely. For much of his life, Admiral Bennett had taken orders — from, of course, progressively fewer. He had obeyed them, whatever he thought. For the rest of his active career, he had given orders, to increasing numbers, and they were obeyed, whatever the recipients thought of them. His was, had always been, a world of seniors and juniors, fixed in place.

The two large men looked frostily at each other, and both waited.

It is, Heimrich thought, all a little ridiculous. It is, however, apparently necessary.

It was, clearly, a question of which would speak next. It hung there for some seconds. And it was Vice Admiral Bennett who spoke.

"I take it," he said, "you know your job. Or — think you do."

It was not much; it was enough. Heimrich smiled faintly.

"Yes, admiral," he said. "I think I do."

For further seconds, the admiral looked at him.

"You may," he said then, "be right. So — carry on."

It was permission granted — at any rate, the form of that. The form didn't matter.

"I want," Heimrich said, "to find out everything I can about your daughter, admiral. Everything you can tell me. I'm — sorry to ask."

"You can belay that," Admiral Bennett said. "She was a fine girl. Everything I could —" For an instant the firm voice slowed, almost broke. "Could have asked," Bennett said, his voice firm again. "Married to a good officer. Where is he?"

He was, Heimrich said, supposed to be on his way there, from some place undesignated, but apparently not distant. Bennett nodded. "Know his duties are very hush-hush," he said.

"There's an Intelligence lieutenant more or less riding herd," Heimrich said.

Bennett looked at Alan Kelley.

"Reserve, sir," Alan said, to which Admiral Bennett, in a certain way, said, "Oh."

Heimrich waited.

"Well," Admiral Bennett said, "what do you want to know? Specifically?"

It always came to that. That was always, in the nature of things, unanswerable.

"Anything that might help," he said. "The usual thing, naturally. Is there anything in her past which would explain what happened? Give a hint of why it happened?"

"No," Bennett said. "This — psychopath? You don't accept him?"

"Say I don't stop with him," Heimrich said. He looked at Dorcas Cameron, who was sitting in a chair, watching, listening. At the admiral's question there was a quickening in her eyes. At Heimrich's answer, the eyes were quenched again. Heimrich waited.

"You're inexact," Bennett told him.

"Now admiral," Heimrich said. "Mine's an inexact occupation. You might say, we navigate most of the time in fog. Without charts. Anything about your daughter. Where, for example, did she go to school?"

It was inevitable that Bennett should say, frosty again, that he could not see what that could have to do with it. It was inevitable that Heimrich, patiently, said he had no idea; that there was no reason to suppose it had any. It was a place to start.

"A good many places," Bennett said. "We lived a good many places — my wife and Carry and I. My wife's dead. Now we're —" He stopped again. He did not go on immediately; he sat down in a terrace chair. He said, "Sit down, Heimrich," courteously, abstractedly, giving permission.

"An American school in Paris," Bennett said. "She was just a child then. A school in Honolulu. College in California for the first two years and then the University of Missouri. Journalism. I never did know why but — it was her life." Again he stopped, again the gray eyes were momentarily shuttered. "Married Wilkins a few years ago," Bennett said. "None of this is any good to you."

"Since then?"

Bennett shook his head.

"Living where they sent him. Recently here

174

with Dorcas," he said. "Wilkins, when he could get here. I know nothing about that — except from her letters. Seemed happy. Complained that her husband was usually somewhere else. Navy wives have cause for that. Part of what they take on."

"There wasn't anything," Dorcas said. "Not since we've been here. Just — ordinary things."

"What you're getting at," Bennett told Heimrich, "is — it was something that started in the past. Somebody she knew in the past."

"I don't know," Heimrich said. "It usually is. There is usually a reason somewhere. Unless killing is a mistake. Or, an insanity. Something a person knows or has or does — something that endangers another person, or denies another person. Money, sometimes. Dangerous knowledge."

"Not money," Bennett said. "Oh — Carry had money. Her mother had a good deal. Her will divided it between Carry and me. But — not money. It will go to her husband, I suppose."

"Yes," Heimrich said. "It goes to her husband, admiral."

"So," Bennett said, "that's out."

He said it simply, as a simple, entirely incontrovertible fact. His life, Heimrich thought, must be largely composed of such incontrovertible facts, must long have been. It must be a comfortable way to live, if one did not know that it was precarious.

"There was never any other man?" Heimrich asked, since he had to. He looked at Dorcas, who shook her head. He looked at the admiral.

"I don't like that question, Heimrich," Admiral Bennett said. Frost was in his eyes again; his eyes said, "Erase that."

Heimrich sighed. He said, "Nevertheless, admiral."

"Carry wasn't like that," Dorcas said, and spoke quickly, impetuously. "Not at all like that."

Another incontrovertible fact. But Dorcas Cameron was, of course, very young.

"Well, admiral?" Heimrich said.

Admiral Bennett looked at him, and the look was a reprimand. Heimrich closed his eyes briefly, and opened them, and waited.

"Dorcas is quite right," Bennett said. "Since Carry married Wilkins, I doubt if she's looked at —" He did not finish.

"Very well," Heimrich said. "Before that." He waited another second or two. "It is quite evident there was, admiral," he said. "That you've remembered something."

"Long time ago," Bennett said. "Got nothing to do with this. Couldn't have."

"Now admiral," Heimrich said. "How do we know that? Another man, obviously. And — it couldn't have been too long ago, could it? Your daughter was a young woman. About — twenty-five, wasn't it?"

"Twenty-six," Bennett said. He considered Heimrich further, made up his mind. "Very well," he said. "When she was twenty, at the university — Missouri University — she met this — young pup. Wrong kind. Mongrel pup. But — nothing would do. I was in Washington. Her mother was dead. She — lacked judgment. All over and done with." The admiral paused and again, momentarily, the sharp gray eyes were shuttered. "No need to say that, was there?" he said. "Since — everything is."

"This man —" Heimrich began, and Bennett did not seem to hear him, or want to wait for him.

"Married him," Bennett said. "Thoroughly nasty specimen, the pup was. After her money, of course. She — she thanked me, Heimrich." He looked at Heimrich sharply. "In so many words," he said.

"For?"

"Paying him off," Bennett said. "Convincing him he'd better take a bird in the hand, since — well, all she got was the income until she was twenty-one. And, I controlled it. It didn't take much argument, Heimrich.

Walked off with the money, all right and she sued him. Desertion is enough, thereabouts."

"And," Heimrich said, "she thanked you?"

"Later on," Bennett said. "Not much later on. Yes. Since she wasn't stupid."

"He was, what?" Heimrich said. "A fellow student?"

"Yes. You meet all kinds at a big school like that. He was several years older. Time out for his military training, I suppose. Army, probably. Not a type we'd want. Scribbled things. Commie, shouldn't wonder."

The Army was not represented on the pleasant, shady terrace, where nothing was really pleasant any more. Heimrich thought it was probably just as well. He supposed Admiral Bennett meant the "mongrel pup" who had been Caroline Bennett's first husband had been a writer, or had wanted to be one; he supposed that the word "Commie" was no more than a handy stick, and that it didn't greatly matter, in any case. He supposed that none of it mattered. Most of what one turned up with didn't. He heard the telephone ringing in the house.

"Very well, Kelley," Admiral Bennett said. "Get that."

"Sir," Alan Kelley said, and went to answer the telephone.

A Volkswagen turned into the driveway

and began to hop up it. Lieutenant Howard Nelson, clearly, was returning. It was to be hoped with news.

"Professor Brinkley, captain," Alan Kelley said, through the screen of the french doors. "Wonders if you've got a minute. Says it's not important if you haven't."

"Thanks, lieutenant," Heimrich said. "Do you mind telling him I'll call back?"

Lieutenant Nelson unraveled himself from the little car. He came across to the terrace, shaking his head. He stopped, looked at the admiral, looked at the Navy car.

"Admiral Bennett?" Nelson said. "Sir, I can't tell you —"

"No," Bennett said. "You can't. You're this Intelligence officer?"

"Sir," Nelson said.

Bennett looked at his left hand. No ring. Involuntarily, Nelson looked at it, too. He started to put it in his pocket, and thought better of that.

"You're supposed to turn up the commander, as I understand it," Bennett said. "Well?"

"Something went wrong with the 'copter, sir," Nelson said. "Had to turn back. Got another one standing by and —"

"Fly boys," Bennett said. "Anything else?"

"No sir," Nelson said, and ceased, for the

admiral, to exist. The admiral turned back to Heimrich, who had started to get up from his chair, planning to call Walter Brinkley back.

"This man Beale —" Admiral Bennett said, and stopped because, half out of his chair, Heimrich had stopped moving. Heimrich sat down again.

"Beale?" he said.

"Beale," Bennett repeated, with emphasis. "The man we were talking about. The puppy who married —"

"Oh," Heimrich said, "you hadn't mentioned his name, admiral."

"Conrad Beale," Bennett said. "Kind of name you'd expect, isn't it? Went out to Hollywood after he got paid off. Place you'd expect him to go. Probably still there."

Why probably still there, Heimrich wondered — why, after half a dozen years, "probably" anywhere? But that was not really what made Captain Heimrich sit, again, firmly in the terrace chair. Beale? With a faulty telephone connection, "Peel"?

"What kind of a looking man was he?" Heimrich asked.

"Black hair," Bennett said. "Spindly sort. Army hadn't done much to set him up. Put him in the Marine Corps, now, and —"

Black hair. Spindly sort. A man in a battered

car, driving away from the Craig house — where he had unsuccessfully attempted to sell brushes to Margo Craig — he had had black hair. Glimpsed, briefly, he had appeared to be thin — tall and thin. Or, if one preferred, spindly. Of course, thousands of men had black hair, carried little weight. And —

"Captain," Dorcas Cameron said. They looked at her. She was not so quenched, now. She leaned forward in her chair and, as she did so, a shaft of sunlight, finding its way through leaves, glinted on her hair. "That's the name of a man who called up a few days ago — Friday, I think it was. I'm sure he said his name was Conrad Beale."

"Unlikely," Admiral Bennett said. "Very unlikely, child. Man's on the West Coast. Probably writing some of this trash you —"

"Admiral," Heimrich said, in a tone which made Admiral Bennett look at him in astonishment.

"Oh," Admiral Bennett said. "Sorry, Heimrich." And that astonished Heimrich.

"Called up, Miss Cameron?" Heimrich said. "About what?"

"Our subscribing to a magazine," Dorcas Cameron said. "One I'd never heard of. We were —"

She and Carry had just sat down to dinner when the telephone rang. Dorcas had answered it. The man had said, "Mrs. Wilkins?" and Dorcas had said it was not, and asked who was calling.

"The *Shakeup!*" he said — she was sure he said, however improbable it sounded. "The magazine," he had said then. "My name is Beale — Conrad Beale. We're making a special offer to new —"

"No," Dorcas said. "We take more magazines than we can read. I'm sorry and —"

"Miss," he said, "can I speak to Mrs. Wilkins? Might be she —"

"I told him no," Dorcas told Heimrich, leaning forward in her chair, the sunlight on her hair. "I hung up and went back and told Carry" — her voice quavered at the name — "told Carry it was just a man trying to sell magazine subscriptions. And we finished dinner."

"Miss Cameron," Heimrich said, "you didn't mention the man's name to your cousin? That he called himself Beale?"

"No," she said. "It — it didn't matter."

Which was obvious.

"He didn't call back?"

"Not when I was there," she said. "Of course —"

And that was obvious, too. Conrad Beale, unsuccessful seller of magazine subscriptions — and of brushes? — might have telephoned again when it was Caroline Wilkins's turn to answer the telephone, or when Dorcas was at her desk in the city. It would have been a coincidence — a preposterous coincidence — if a Conrad Beale had telephoned the former wife of a Conrad Beale by chance only, to sell her a subscription only.

"Sir," Lieutenant Nelson said, addressing the senior officer present.

Admiral Bennett looked at him as if he had never seen him before. He said, however, "Well, Nelson?"

"We had occasion to investigate a magazine called *Shakeup!*" Nelson said. "In connection with — a restricted matter, sir. It's what is called a scandal sheet, sir. That is, it —"

"Nelson!" Admiral Bennett said. "I know what a scandal sheet is. Precisely the sort of thing I'd expect a man like Beale to wind up connected with." He turned to Heimrich. "See what kind of a man he is, Heimrich?"

"Sir," Nelson said, and waited to be spoken to. He was snorted at, but snorted at permissively.

"This man Beale," Nelson said. "He is — one of the editors, sir. Not a subscription solicitor. At least I shouldn't —"

"Very well, Nelson," Admiral Bennett said. "Er — thank you, Nelson."

"Thank you, sir," Lieutenant Howard Nelson said.

Bennett looked at him with renewed frost. He snorted at Lieutenant Nelson, who thought, How the hell *do* you get along with the trade school boys?

# X

This magazine called *Shakeup!* — a designation it apparently lived up to fully — had been in existence for something over three years. Its illustrations went as far as postal regulations would tolerate and its text flirted as playfully with the laws of libel. (It had, as a matter of fact, had to settle once. It appeared that the movie starlet in question — very much in question — had been demonstrably in London at the time.) Half a dozen more libel suits were pending against it. But such suits often pend indefinitely. There were, it was suspected, still other aspects to the operation of *Shakeup!* The problem there was that the blackmailed are often reticent.

Heimrich and Sergeant Forniss sat, over drinks, in the barroom of the Maples Inn. (The Maples Inn preferred the designation "cocktail lounge.") Forniss, having enquired, reported. Heimrich knew the racket.

"Set up in type," Forniss said. "Proofed. Proofs sent to subject with the notation that the enclosed article, in which he — usually she, probably — may be interested is to appear in an early issue. If subject has changes to

185

suggest, the editors will be glad to discuss them with him. Maybe something about the expense already incurred in collecting the material and so forth. In case subject is outstandingly dumb."

"Any squeals?"

That, of course, was it. Subjects seldom squealed. They reimbursed *Shakeup!* for expenses incurred. Or they said, Publish and be sued.

"One or two squeals —" Forniss said. "Nothing they could make stick." "They" being the city police.

"Beale?"

Conrad Beale was an associate editor, one of three. The executive editor was one Oliver Felson. "Got him once on a shakedown," Forniss said. "Six–seven years ago. Suspended sentence. Nothing since."

"Beale?"

"Nope," Forniss said. "Nothing on him. He wasn't at the office, of course. No idea where Mr. Beale could be reached, they hadn't. Begins to look like the old man's off the hook, doesn't it? But — he was there. Saw something that scared him."

"Or," Heimrich said, "shocked him. It does look like it, Charlie."

"Be a relief to the girl," Forniss said, and emptied his glass. "She's taking it hard." He considered his empty glass. "Harder than you'd figure," he said, to the glass. "Makes you wonder whether —" He did not say what it made him wonder, or need to.

"I don't know, Charlie," Heimrich said. "An ugly thing to come on. Particularly when you were all — lighted up. As she must have been. And then to feel that, if you'd tried a little harder, done a little more, there wouldn't have been that to come on. With, we'll have to admit, some reason."

"Actually," Forniss said. "Not much."

"Now Charlie," Heimrich said. "Perhaps not, actually. Everything can be explained away. She asked somebody who should have known and — got bad advice. If she did. But, things like that happen inside people, Charlie. Especially people as young as she is. I don't think it's anything more than that. Anyway, she was in New York at the time, with Kelley. At the Municipal Building."

Forniss looked at Heimrich and raised his eyebrows.

"Yes," Heimrich said. "I asked them to check. They were there, as stated."

"So," Forniss said. "The husband came back, they tell me."

Lieutenant Commander Brady Wilkins had come back — come at a little before six, with a face all strained tendons, hard lines, with eyes blank. He had answered what Heimrich asked in a voice without expression. He had known of no reason anyone might have for killing Caroline. He had never heard of Ashley Adams; he had known, of course, of "the place" where the girls lay in the sun. Once or twice, he and Caroline had gone there together. His voice remained expressionless, although — Heimrich thought — the memory of those times in the sun, and of her slender beauty then, must have been almost unbearable. He knew Caroline had been married before, and to a man named Beale and that the fact had "worried" her. There had been no reason it should. It had made no difference. He had never met Beale.

Wilkins had been, during the short questioning, neither patient nor impatient. In a sense, he had not been there at all. Only the shell of him was there. Brady Wilkins did not, Heimrich thought, care where the shell was, or what happened to it.

Where had he been from the time, on Monday, when he had left his wife and Alan Kelley at Grand Central was not pin-pointed. Wilkins had been asked.

"Now wait a minute, captain," Lieutenant Nelson, who was sitting in, said, in a great hurry. Admiral Bennett looked at him; Heimrich looked at him. Commander Wilkins looked at nothing; merely waited; was somewhere far away, the shell of him left behind.

"Sir," Nelson said, and flushed slightly. "My orders, sir —"

Admiral Bennett snorted.

"In general, commander," Heimrich said.

"I had certain people to see on Long Island," Brady Wilkins said. "I can't be more explicit."

Heimrich could guess. There are Defense Department suppliers on Long Island. Presumably, some of the things they supply are secret things. He did not guess aloud.

"All the same," Sergeant Forniss said, having been brought up to date — "all the same, it could be a — convenience."

"As you said this morning, Charlie."

"It's still true," Forniss said. "In the abstract. Better than the old one — the lady's reputation gimmick. And — he gets the money. And — could be Mrs. Wilkins had a date with her former husband yesterday morning. Could be the commander happened to come home unexpectedly. Found them together. Got — upset."

"And killed his wife," Heimrich said. "Not bothering with Beale." Forniss started to say something. "I know, Charlie," Heimrich said. "I can think of explanations, too. We'll know more when we pick up Beale."

"Funny he wants to get in touch with you," Forniss said. "Funny he doesn't if he wants to. If he was the one who called."

"Yes," Heimrich said. "We'll ask him that too when we find him."

"And," Forniss said, "what he had on Mrs. Wilkins. That he thought she might be willing to pay for. That sort of thing's his racket."

"Yes," Heimrich said. "Probably it is. Carrying on his trade, it looks like. And that the admiral's right — Beale's a mongrel pup. You'd expect him to be the one rubbed out, wouldn't you? Not the girl. However —"

He turned toward the bar and held up two fingers. The bartender, pleased, nodded at him. He brought drinks. With them, he brought canapés. "Damn," Captain Heimrich said. "That reminds me."

Forniss looked at him.

"Canapés," Heimrich said. "Cocktail party. Walter Brinkley. He has something he wants to tell me."

Heimrich found the telephone, in an aperture. He found Walter Brinkley's telephone number and dialed it and waited and was told that this was Professor Brinkley's residence.

"Heimrich," he said. "Could I speak to Mr. Brinkley?"

" 'Fraid not, cap'n," Harry Washington said, adjusting his accent. "Professor, he's in New York. Dinner for somebody at the Faculty Club. Won't be back till pretty late, seems like. I's sorry, suh. Mighty sorry."

"All right," Heimrich said. "He asked me to call him back. Tell him I called, will you? And that I'll call again in the morning?"

"I sho will, cap'n," Harry said. "I'll sho do that."

Heimrich went back to the table. They finished their drinks. They went into the dining room for dinner. It was eight-thirty when Mrs. Lambert, who owned the inn, came to their table and said that there was a telephone call for Captain Heimrich.

"— overemphasis that will inevitably result in communication entirely by mathematical formulae," Abel Milner, exaggerating by intention, said with emphasis, and leaned forward in his chair in the lounge of the Men's Faculty Club of Dyckman University. "With the further result that —"

Walter Brinkley listened, with as much of his mind as he could spare, to Abel Milner, Ph.D., associate professor of English Literature. The collar of Milner's dinner jacket gaped excessively as Milner leaned forward. Poor Milner had only his salary, and a wife and two children. A brilliant young man, all the same — a man only in his early fifties

191

and already with several admirable publications. A good ten years from emeritus. Walter Brinkley, supporting a cocktail glass on the arm of his chair, nodded his head thoughtfully. But he was not, save fractionally, thinking of what Abel Milner was saying. Brinkley was thinking, primarily, that he really should try once more to get in touch with Captain M. L. Heimrich.

Looked at in one way, Brinkley thought and nodded his head again, and then finished his drink — looked at in one way, he had made every effort which could properly be expected to get in touch with his friend Heimrich. Looked at in another, what he had to tell — to suggest, rather — was of such negligible importance that only a fussy old man (a professor; face it) would think it at all worth passing on. Looked at in another, what he should be thinking of was the few remarks with which, as toastmaster, he would (after delicately knocking on the rim of his water glass with the edge of a knife) introduce to assembled professors (all of whom knew him very well) Professor Francis Anderson (dear old Andy) who had, as of the end of the just-completed semester, retired as head of the English Department. Welcome to the ranks of the emeritus —

"Thank you, Fergus," Walter Brinkley said

to a club servant, accepting another martini. One more, he trusted, would dull his appetite sufficiently. Confronted by the food of the Men's Faculty Club of Dyckman University, one sought dulled appetite. Walter Brinkley sighed.

"Precisely," Abel Milner said, and leaned even further forward. "The outlook, Walter, is appalling. There is no other word for it."

"None," Walter Brinkley said. "None at all, Abel."

It was such a tiny thing, a thing of so little importance. The proper course was to forget it entirely. Or, if not entirely, at least for the time being. Tomorrow would be time enough to offer to Heimrich — who would be polite; who would undoubtedly be tolerant — the tiny fact, or theory (it was no more than that) which had lodged in the meshes of Walter Brinkley's mind as, having garaged his car after his lunch with the Misses Monroe, he stood at the kitchen sink and let water run cold for drinking.

Brinkley looked at his watch. Eight-fifteen. Fifteen minutes, then, before the assembled professors departed reluctantly from the comfort of the lounge — how the same club could sustain so admirable a bar and so depressing a kitchen had been a matter of general and gloomy speculation for some twenty years —

and entered the dining room. Just time enough to give it one more try.

Walter Brinkley finished his drink and snapped his fingers, in the gesture of a man who has just thought of something too long forgotten. Abel Milner stopped. "Telephone call I damn near forgot," Brinkley said, and shook his head — in the gesture of an ancient whose memory fails — and went to a telephone booth in the hall outside the lounge. By leaving the door open and sticking his head out occasionally, he could see the beginning of the exodus.

Fortunately, he had coins. He started with the police barracks in Hawthorne. The barracks answered quickly, but at a subordinate level. Transfer took time; minutes ebbed. A less subordinate level had to check, and that took time, also. Captain M. L. Heimrich was, at last reports, at the Maples Inn in North Wellwood.

"Thank you," Walter Brinkley said, and hung up, and immediately realized that the police barracks would have had available the telephone number of the Maples Inn, which he, now, could not remember. It was written down, clearly, in a black book of telephone numbers frequently called and that book, on the downstairs telephone table, Brinkley could clearly visualize. The book, not the number.

Brinkley stuck his head out of the telephone booth. The exodus had started. Professors stood, making final remarks to one another, putting glasses down. A few minutes only — as toastmaster, he could not be tardy.

He put a dime in and dialed Operator. He asked and was told; for out of town numbers, he should dial 211. His dime came back, and was reinserted. The lounge was, without any doubt, emptying.

"North what, please?" "Well*ford?* Oh — Well*wood.* So sorry. One moment please."

Brinkley stuck his head out again. It was noticed by Professor Abel Milner. Milner beckoned; Brinkley nodded the exposed head briskly.

"The number is —" the operator said. "Thank you," Brinkley said. "Will you get it for me?"

"Certainly," the operator said, and the telephone made sounds. Abel Milner hovered in the doorway between dining room and lounge. He looked at Walter Brinkley with evident anxiety.

The telephone produced further sounds. It produced the busy signal.

"I'm sorry, sir," the operator said. "The line is busy. Shall I try again in —"

Brinkley put the receiver back. He went out

of booth and across lounge, at a pace just under a trot.

For which, subsequently, he blamed himself, at first excessively. But with the facts assembled, it was not — was obviously not — true that if he had kept on trying he might have saved a life.

"Heimrich speaking," Heimrich said.

The man's voice was one Heimrich had never heard before. It was rather high-pitched. The man spoke quickly.

"My name's Beale," the man said. "I've been trying to get you."

"Yes," Heimrich said. "Conrad Beale?"

"All right," Beale said. "Gather they've filled you in. Yes. Former husband of Carry Wilkins. I suppose you've got the bloodhounds out?"

"Now Mr. Beale," Heimrich said. "Why?"

"Went by to see her that morning," Beale said. "Happened to be in the neighborhood —" He stopped suddenly. "Not convincing, is it?" he said.

"Not the last," Heimrich said. "No. Where are you, Mr. Beale?"

"About —" Beale said, but then, "Never mind. I'm not trying to run out."

"Good," Heimrich said.

"I think maybe I can give you a lead," Beale

said. "Not sure but — maybe. You'll give me a break?"

"If you had anything —"

"Oh for God's sake," Beale said. "I don't mean that. You'll listen to what I've got to tell you? If it turns out there is something?"

"Naturally," Heimrich said.

"Tell you what," Beale said. "I'll come there — to the inn. Anyway I've got a room there. O.K.?"

"Yes," Heimrich said. "How soon?"

"Oh," Beale said. "Give me half an hour. I'll —"

There was, faintly, a clicking sound on the line. But then Beale spoke again.

"Not longer than half an hour," he said. "Pick you up in the lounge?"

"Yes," Heimrich said, and listened to Beale hang up a telephone.

Beale was, as he said, staying at the inn. He had a room in what the inn called The Annex, where a good many permanent residents — permanent and for the most part aged — stayed. He had not telephoned from his room. The call had come from outside.

The suggestion of a passkey ruffled Mrs. Lambert, which Heimrich could understand, could sympathize with. He unruffled her, gently. Forniss went to see what of interest there might be in Conrad Beale's room, and Conrad Beale would never know he had — unless there was reason he should know.

Heimrich waited. He waited in the cocktail lounge. A reporter found him there and advanced with enthusiasm. "No," Heimrich said. "Nothing new. You'll know when there is."

The reporter tried. He failed. He ordered a drink and took it with him — took it, Heimrich supposed, to set beside a typewriter. Several typewriters clicked in the inn. Heimrich, faintly, could hear them through open windows as he waited. He could also hear a whippoorwill, tearing holes in silence.

Heimrich had waited fifteen minutes or so when Forniss came back. He came fast, with something to tell.

"Somebody — " Forniss said and the night roared — roared once and then again.

The sound came from outside the inn; it seemed to come from everywhere outside the inn. A shotgun, barrels fired in quick succession, can gash the silence of a rural night — blast it into fragments. Heimrich and Forniss were running toward the inn's door while the sound of the explosions still echoed. And then, on wooden floor, wooden stairs, of the old inn many feet clattered.

A porch stretched the front of the inn, with

steps leading down from it at either end and wider steps toward the street. Forniss ran left on the porch, his feet heavy on boards. Heimrich went right, went down the steps at the end to the driveway which led toward the rear of the building, toward the parking lot. One way seemed as good as another, and Heimrich ran down the sloping drive toward the lot.

There was one light on a post in the lot, and it seemed to make more shadows than it made light. There were half a dozen cars — dark cars. Nothing there, Heimrich thought and stopped and listened, and heard a sound.

It was human; a human made it, trying to speak, to call out. There were no words in the sound; the sound was choked, meaningless. And horrible — a bubbling sound.

Heimrich went toward the sound.

The man spilled from the open door of a car, shoulders inside, lower body hanging down. It was as if somebody, something, had started to pour him from the car. Heimrich took two strides across the center of the lot and a car leaped at him from the side. The car had no lights, was a hurtling blackness.

Heimrich threw himself to the side — threw himself from his feet, caught himself on his hands and rolled on rough pavement. For an instant he could feel one of the car's tires brush his feet.

He rolled to his knees and had his revolver in his hand and there was no use in that.

The car had not gone up the drive he had run down. It had gone on toward the rear of the lot and, there, plunged suddenly into blackness.

A big car — but even that was a guess. Any car, hurtling out of darkness, is big enough. A car, at a guess, itself dark in color. And — gone, now.

Gone and, Heimrich knew within seconds, left death behind. Nobody could live who was so hurt.

The man, the tall thin man, the black-haired man, had caught both charges in the chest. And yet, when Heimrich reached toward him, began to lower him to the ground — it didn't matter what one did with him — he was still alive. His eyes were alive and saw Heimrich — saw him for an instant. In that instant the man — the dead man still alive — tried to speak again. But words did not come from his lips, only blood. And then the dead man was dead.

Forniss ran down the driveway and then, out of darkness, there were others. One of the others was a photographer and there was a sudden, blinding flash of light. The light was enough to show the photographer he had a picture he couldn't print.

"All right," Forniss said, in a cop's hardest voice. "Get back."

But that didn't matter, either. Heimrich stood up.

"Beale?" Forniss said.

"I suppose so," Heimrich said. He looked around at those who formed a half circle, who stared. One of them was the bartender.

"You," Heimrich said. "You recognize him?"

"Mr. Beale," the bartender said. "Oh God!" He stepped forward a pace and looked down at the dead man. He moved backward more quickly and turned away, and then took several uncertain steps toward the edge of the lot.

They got it started then; got started the slow and patient compilation of the facts of murder. A motorcycle trooper was the first there, and then they could leave the body under guard and get on with it.

The car which had lurched at Heimrich had gone down a narrow passageway between the main building and the annex of the Maples Inn and, beyond it, to an alley which led to a street. Presumably, its lights had gone on then and it had gone — wherever its driver wanted it to go. There was nothing to go on.

No license number. License plates do not show on a dark car. No identification as to make or model. There had not been time for that.

"Got here first," Heimrich said. "Parked and waited. Got out when Beale got here and, at a guess, walked over. Probably not showing the gun. It's pretty dim light." Beale had started to get out of the car and the gun had roared at him, from very close. The murderer had gone back to his own car and started the motor and then, it was to be assumed, heard Heimrich's feet on the drive and — waited. When Heimrich was in range, the driver had tried again, with a different weapon. No luck this time, but it had been close.

"Damn close," Heimrich told Forniss, and they walked back up the drive to the inn. "You found something in his room?"

"In a way," Forniss said. "That somebody else had been looking. Forced the door. Anybody could do it — with a nail file, damn near. Prized his suitcase open, went through what I guess was his other suit — hanging in the closet, that was. Turned the pockets out and left the suit on the floor. In a hurry. So — we'll have to have it printed before we look ourselves."

Which was obvious; which took more time. There were ways to fill it. Item: Young Ash

Adams said his father was in his room, and locked in it. Which was conclusive — if they took Young Ash's word. And — took his word his father could not drive a car.

Dorcas Cameron and Lieutenant Kelley, and Admiral Bennett, were at the Wilkins house. (The old Adams house.) Commander Wilkins was not; had not been since a little after six — since, in fact, a few minutes after Heimrich had talked to him. He had gone to the undertaker's to do those things — those necessary, meaningless, agonizing things — which have to be done, and had been left waiting for him to do. He had gone alone because he had wanted to go alone. He had not returned. The admiral had gone earlier in the afternoon and looked at the unscarred face of his dead child.

They would have to check, of course — check the time of Wilkins's arrival, of his —

"Better give them a ring, Charlie," Heimrich said, and Forniss called the undertaker's. Commander Wilkins had reached there at about six-thirty. Certain formalities had required some ten minutes. They had taken him, then, to the room his wife's body lay in. He had stayed there, alone, for perhaps half an hour.

"Funny thing about the commander," Forniss said. "Always seems to be somewhere else but — where?"

There was that, admittedly.

Joe Parks, on the other hand, was readily come by. He was in a tavern, and he had been there for two hours — a considerable part of which he had devoted to rather loud comment on Paul Craig (the bastard). But there was no longer much reason, if there had ever been, to count Parks in.

Conrad Beale had checked into the Maples Inn Monday evening. He had had a suitcase and a typewriter, and had wanted — for four or five days, at an estimate — a quiet room where the sound of typing wouldn't bother other people. That had got him a corner room in the annex.

"Poor Mr. Simpkins almost never uses his hearing aid," Mrs. Lambert said. "So it seemed like a good place. He's in the next room, you know."

Those who had rooms in the annex did not, leaving it, pass through the main lobby of the inn, so that Beale could have come and gone as he chose and done both unobserved. Which was possibly, of course, the idea.

And, among many uncertainties, one special one remained unresolved. Neither Heimrich nor Forniss, after looking carefully at Beale's body, could be sure that he was the "brush salesman" who had driven away from Paul

Craig's monstrous house, after failing to sell his wares to Margo Craig. On the other hand, they could not be sure that he was not.

"What it comes to," Forniss said, "there's no shape to the damn thing."

"Now Charlie," Heimrich said. "One we don't see. Yet."

But that, Charles Forniss thought, came to much the same thing.

The fingerprint men finished. They had found Beale's prints, and those of a woman. The woman had been established as one of the maids. The maid had certainly not — the very idea! — gone through Beale's things. If they thought she was that kind of girl — then tears of indignation.

"Gloves," Forniss said, "are the invention of the devil."

The room was comfortable, comfortably furnished. There was a portable typewriter on a table and a typewriter case under it. There was typewriter paper in the case, and a dozen letterhead sheets, which proved that Conrad Beale had, indeed, been an associate editor of *Shakeup!* Unfortunately, nothing was typed on any of the sheets, nor was there anything in the wastebasket.

There was no doubt that the room had been searched by someone. It appeared that the searcher was looking for anything there was to be found — for things big enough to go in bureau drawers, small enough to go in watch pockets. Perhaps, then, not for one special thing.

The suitcase had been emptied on the floor and its contents — shirts and socks and underwear, used and unused — left there. The shirts had laundry marks, now duly noted; the typewriter was an Underwood, fairly recent model. Heimrich typed the usual lines — that the party needed aid, that the brown fox was lively as ever.

The "o" was out of line. The upper case "M" had a nick in it.

They were quick and they were expert and they were thorough, as experts are. It was Forniss who found the photograph, investigating an apparently accidental rip in the lining of the suitcase. The photograph was under the lining — a snapshot, and not a recent one; a somewhat faded one.

The photograph was of two people — of a girl in a bathing suit; a slender, rather tall girl, with curled blond hair; a very young girl. She stood beside, had an arm around, a broad and apparently affable man, clearly much older than she, who wore trunks and who was quite remarkably muscular, and whose broad chest bore three scars — bullet scars. The man looked very pleased with himself.

They looked at the photograph. They looked at each other.

"Yep," Forniss said. "Not much doubt about it."

"No," Heimrich said. "Not much doubt. Imagine meeting The Dutchman here."

# XI

The girl in the snapshot — which had to have been made some years before, since Homer (The Dutchman) Schneider had been dead for some years — might, Heimrich and Forniss agreed, be any pretty girl. Any pretty blond girl.

"Mrs. Wilkins was blond," Forniss pointed out. "She had pretty much the same kind of figure."

The girl in the photograph was, at a guess, in her middle teens — at a guess, sixteen or so. She had regular features — regular and pretty and softly young; she had a face which had not firmed into pattern. (But also she was squinting a little against the sun, and the photograph was somewhat faded and not too sharply focused to begin with.)

"Ten years ago," Forniss said, "The Dutchman was still around. Ten years ago Mrs. Wilkins would have been — what? Sixteen?"

"Yes," Heimrich said. "And — going to school in Honolulu. Or, California."

Forniss raised his eyebrows slightly.

"All right, Charlie," Heimrich said. "I didn't get it year by year, obviously. We will, naturally. What do you remember about The Dutchman, Charlie?"

"Big-time punk," Forniss said. "Ten, fifteen years ago. In K.C., mostly. Got taken care of in —" He stopped; he shrugged. "It was quite a while ago," Forniss said. "And a long way off."

Which was the point, and the problem. The heavy, affable face of the late Homer Schneider was unforgettable, particularly to policemen. Policemen watched for his affable face and, whenever and wherever it appeared, took suitable precautions, since the only thing affable about The Dutchman was his face. But he had not appeared, or at any rate not been noticed, often in the East.

"I don't remember," Forniss said, "that we ever had a run-in with Mr. Schneider. Headache to the boys out West. Unless he happened to be a meal ticket. Doubt whether we've got much dope on him."

Heimrich nodded his head slowly, and took a last look at the photograph and put it in his pocket.

"You know, Charlie," he said, "I think I'll take a run into town."

Again, Forniss raised his eyebrows.

"Yes," Heimrich said, "to check a little. They'll have plenty. And — I don't know exactly why, Charlie. As you say, there's nothing to show he fits in at all. An entirely different iron our friend Beale had in the fire, very likely. May be a waste of time, as you say."

Forniss had, he decided, said a good deal by raising his eyebrows. Not, when he thought of it, that he hadn't meant to.

"May have nothing to do with the pattern, naturally," Heimrich said, and was, Forniss decided, talking largely to himself. "But, if he has he — rather sticks out, doesn't he? Nice private murder and all at once The Dutchman. And some of the punks out there had quite a way with shotguns, Charlie."

"Yep," Forniss said. "Only, he's dead. You don't argue he isn't dead?"

"The evil that men do," Heimrich said. "No, I don't argue he isn't dead. I think I'll go into town all the same. Suppose you get a picture of our friend Beale — nice clean picture. The face is all right. One of the boys has got one of these developing cameras, probably. Show it around a little?"

"Yep," Forniss said. "In a nice way? If they happen to be up and about?"

"By all means, Charlie," Heimrich said. "Nicest way possible. Tomorrow, if it's more convenient for everybody. I'll be back before then, naturally."

Heimrich, for no reason he could think of, drove into New York rather faster than is his custom. There is usually no great hurry in checking on the past of a dead man. But Heimrich does not, while investigating a case, like bodies to accumulate.

Centre Street had a good deal on Schneider, Homer; alias "The Dutchman," alias several other things. Centre Street had photographs, all better than the snapshot, although in none of them did Schneider look especially pleased with himself. In most of which he was wearing numbers. Centre Street had fingerprints, and history.

Schneider had been born in 1905, in Chicago. He had begun with the to-be-expected boyish thefts; had come into his own during prohibition, beginning modestly as a truck driver; graduating within a short time to hijacking; proving a handy man with a sawed-off shotgun. (Several arrests, no major convictions.) He had left Chicago for Kansas City not at the request of the police, some of whom were nevertheless grateful, but after a misunderstanding about territories — a misunderstanding into which .45's entered. He had done well in Kansas City, rising rapidly. When prohibition ended, The Dutchman had still found much to occupy his time — gambling, prostitution, narcotics, and the like. The Dutchman did not, Heimrich decided, differ markedly from others in his line of work; he had, however, been more successful than most. This had, it was evident, aroused jealousy here and there; Schneider had been often shot at and several times hit. He had, however, proved unusually bullet-resistant. Heimrich took the snapshot from his pocket and looked at Schneider's scarred chest. Very resistant.

But resistance had finally failed. That had been in 1950. It had been thought that, by then, The Dutchman had retired (with, it was thought, plenty) but it was evident that there had been those who took a different view. The Dutchman had left his real estate office (in which real estate operations had, it appeared, actually been carried on) and got into his car and pressed the starter. Enough fragments had been found to make identification positive. There was no doubt whatever The Dutchman was dead.

He was survived by his wife, Opal. He had left her a substantial sum, although not as substantial as had been expected. Far away and long ago, Heimrich thought; farther from North Wellwood than was at all helpful. Heimrich returned records and expressed thanks and, after a few moments of consideration, drove uptown to the office of the New York *Daily News*. Having come this far from North Wellwood —

The *Daily News* morgue did not have much

about the late Homer Schneider. He appeared in a few news stories as "the notorious gangster" and one of the stories, longer than the rest, had to do with his fragmentation. There was also a feature story, from the Sunday edition — one of a series entitled "The Gangland Era." In it, The Dutchman had split billing with one "Buggsy" Moran.

The story told Heimrich chiefly what he already knew. But, it was illustrated — Schneider, clothed this time, was pictured with a girl also (relatively) clothed. The clipping was old and yellowed; the reproduction a little smudgy. But the girl, again, was very young and pretty, and had regular features — a little exaggeration of feature would have helped. Not surely, but probably, the girl of the snapshot and, if so, Schneider's wife. Heimrich read further. The feature writer corrected his terminology. Schneider's "child bride." Opal Schneider, née Opal Potter.

"Like some others of the period," Heimrich read, " 'The Dutchman,' while ruthless in most respects, had a streak of sentimentality. It was because of this, presumably, that he married Opal — a pretty, but poorly educated orphan of fifteen, a native of Kansas. How they first met was never clear, since Schneider's sphere of activity was urban, and she lived on a run-down farm near Oswego.

Schneider was in his late forties at the time of their marriage.

"After their marriage, Schneider sent his young wife through high school in Kansas City, Missouri, and when he was killed, two years or so after she was graduated, left her an estate estimated at some twenty-five thousand dollars. Opal — her Cinderella party over — dropped from sight for a time after her notorious husband was killed, but is reported later to have attended the state university under another name."

Onward and upward Opal Potter had gone, rather understandably under another name. And I, Heimrich thought, am obviously going nowhere — going down a blind alley leading to nothing. He put the small sheaf of yellowed clippings back in an envelope and, briefly, regarded the envelope. "The state university," not otherwise identified. But, quite possibly — quite probably, even — the university of the state in which she had attended high school. Therefore, the University of Missouri. Why bother with — of course! Caroline Wilkins, when she was Caroline Bennett, had gone there. She had even met Conrad Beale there. And — Opal Schneider, née Potter, alias something else entirely?

Or — For a moment Heimrich shut his eyes, the better to listen to his thoughts. Opal had been slender and blond. So had Caroline Bennett. Schneider's pretty wife, who came, it appeared, from what Heimrich could only think of as the depths of Kansas, would be about the right age. He figured briefly. A few years older. But, within limits, failing close scrutiny, a person's age is what a person says it is. Especially a woman's age. And —

It was tempting. It could have been gone on with. Opal knew something, or had something, which The Dutchman's former associates sought. Opal (now Caroline) had been caught up with, had revealed knowledge, had not paid up, had — It was a temptation which passed, faded, like a wisp of smoke. Caroline Wilkins had been Caroline Bennett, the daughter of Vice Admiral Jonathan Bennett. Any other idea was preposterous. Among other things, the unquestionable existence, the indubitable authenticity, of Admiral Bennett made it so.

That Caroline, while at the University of Missouri, might have known Opal was not, of course, preposterous. It was somewhat unlikely — state universities run large, run in strata. Opal Potter, however improved — and it seemed unlikely that high school and prolonged association with Schneider would have improved her markedly — would remain still on quite a different social plane from that of

Caroline Bennett, the child of the very best Navy, by force of necessity youthful citizen of the world. Still —

And, where did it get him? That Opal had passed along to Caroline, for reasons not to be guessed at, information of perilous value? The answer to that was obvious — "Phooey!" was the answer to that. Forniss had been right in raising eyebrows. The defunct Schneider, his "girl bride" had nothing to do with the case. Beale had been carrying the snapshot for unrelated reasons of his own. So —

Of course, hair can be dyed. Dyed, for example, to a burnished red. Like the hair of the pretty, worried child who would not now (almost certainly would not) have further cause to torment herself. Since it was unlikely that Young Ash was lying about his father. Dorcas Cameron had regular features, of course and — And she was too short by half a dozen inches, and too young by at least as many years. Opal Schneider had been tall; taller, at any rate, than her husband, who had been five feet seven and weighed two hundred and eight pounds. Unless, in the snapshot, she had been standing on something. Heimrich took the snapshot out of his pocket and looked at it again. Another look did not help. The photographer had cut off their feet.

Heimrich got up from the table. He felt

heavy, sluggish. The trouble is, he thought, my mind's stopped. I'm worrying this side issue to give my mind the semblance of movement, to delude myself. It doesn't lie here — in this snapshot, in this old story from far away and years ago. Get back where it does lie, make the mind work; turn back out of this dark alley and —

Blond hair can, of course, be dyed black. Dyed black and curled tightly like the hair of the very handsome, very slender, Margo Craig. At a guess, the age would be right. Skip it, Heimrich told himself. Get back on —

"Have you got an envelope on a man named Paul Craig?" Heimrich asked the morgue attendant, who was listed as the "librarian" and never called that. The morgue attendant went to see; he came back with an envelope which was even thinner than that which had held the yellowed records of The Dutchman's life and death. This, labeled "Craig, Paul," held, in fact, only two clippings.

In one he was an irrelevance. He was a survivor — the survivor of Helen Sibley, the "well-known popular novelist," who had died some years before, after a long illness; who had been, in social life, Mrs. Paul Craig, of Park Avenue and North Wellwood, New York. There were several paragraphs about Helen Sibley, who appeared to have been famous, and to have lapsed from fame, some years before her death.

The other clipping was more recent. It reported the marriage of Paul Craig, "whose first wife was the well-known novelist Helen Sibley," to Miss Margo Nowlin, of Baltimore, daughter of Mr. and Mrs. Thomas Sibley Nowlin. (Craig, Heimrich thought, had ridden into print this time, also, on the train of his first wife's skirt, and brought his second wife with him.)

Craig and Margo Nowlin (who had been doing postgraduate work at Dyckman University at the time they met) had been married in church. Miss Nowlin, a graduate of Goucher College, had been given in marriage by her father, and a sister, Pauline, had been one of her bridesmaids. Mr. and Mrs. Craig had planned to travel extensively before reopening the Craig house in North Wellwood.

So much for dark alleys, so much for wild geese. Heimrich expressed thanks for cooperation supplied and went to the lobby of the News building and found a telephone book. He found that "Felson, Oliver," had an address on West Fifty-seventh Street, and thought of telephoning first and decided against it. There was nothing to indicate that Felson might decide to prove slippery, but there was no particular reason to give him a chance to slip. There was, Heimrich felt, no particular reason to give the editor of *Shakeup!* anything. If Felson was the kind who went to bed early — which seemed improbable — he would be asked to wake up.

Heimrich pushed a doorbell on the seventh floor of an apartment house on West Fifty-seventh. When nothing happened, he continued to press the button. In rather more than due time, a fat man in a silk dressing gown opened the door. He wore a long cigar between two fingers of his right hand. He had eyes which appeared to have no particular color and were set deep in a fat face. Editors of scandal magazines, Heimrich decided, came in all sizes.

"Mr. Felson?" Heimrich said.

The round man said, "Yup."

"The editor of *Shakeup!*?"

"Yup."

"Heimrich, State Police."

The fat man did not say anything. He was not, it was clear, a man who led.

"A man of yours has been killed," Heimrich said, and doubted he was giving information. "A man named Beale."

"Yup," Felson said, and looked at the long cigar. "Heard it on the radio," he said. He looked at Heimrich through pinched-in, colorless eyes. "Identification?"

Heimrich showed him identification. The fat man looked at it very carefully. He gave it back. He said, "Yup. Come on in." Heimrich went on in. Felson sat in a fat chair and drew on his cigar. And waited.

"What was Beale doing up there?" Heimrich said. "In North Wellwood? Where he got killed?"

Felson considered this very carefully. He shook his head. He said, "I wouldn't know."

"Now Mr. Felson," Heimrich said. "Guess, then."

"No guess," Felson said. "Unless he was on the track of something."

Heimrich took his turn at waiting.

"A story, could be," Felson said. "Nothing I know about. Could be he was just visiting friends."

"Who?"

"Nope. I wouldn't know that, either."

"Felson," Heimrich said. "Beale worked for you. If he was on the track, as you say, of a story, you'd know about it."

"You say I would," Felson said. "Doesn't prove I would. Also — aren't you a little off your beat? This is the city. City's got cops."

"Yes," Heimrich said. "Want me to call them in?"

The fat man looked hard at Heimrich from

the fat-pinched eyes. Heimrich looked at him and waited.

"All right," Felson said. "I don't know a damn thing about it. Could be he was working on something, like I said. Something he was developing. Hadn't got enough on to bring up. That's the way we work, captain. Beale, or one of the others, gets on to something. Finds out if it's anything we can use. If he thinks it is — brings it in. That's when I come in."

"Not before?"

"If I get the tip, sure. Otherwise, nope."

"And you're saying you haven't any idea what Beale may have been working on?"

"Nope. For all I know, he was visiting friends."

"Not," Heimrich said, "very friendly friends."

"There's that," Felson said.

"Mr. Felson," Heimrich said. "I think you're lying."

It did not upset Felson in the least. He merely nodded his round head.

"Up to you," Felson said.

"Look at this," Heimrich said, and showed Felson the snapshot, and watched the man look at it. There was not, he found, much to be gained by watching Felson. Neither heavy face nor slitted eyes showed anything whatever. Felson might, for all his face revealed, have been looking at blank paper. He handed the snapshot back.

"Well?" Heimrich said, expecting nothing.

"Nope," Felson said.

"The man," Heimrich said, "was a punk. Operated out in the Middle West. Name of Schneider. They called him The Dutchman. He's been dead for several years."

"So?"

"The girl is — probably is, anyway — his widow. Name of Opal."

This time Felson said nothing at all, but merely looked at Heimrich. If he had any expression, it was one of boredom.

"Beale had it with him," Heimrich said. "The snapshot. Hidden in the lining of his suitcase."

"All right," Felson said. "He had it with him."

"If the girl's alive," Heimrich said. "Doesn't want it known, say, that she used to be the wife of this punk. Picture might be worth something, mightn't it?"

"If she was prominent enough," Felson said. "Might be a story in it. Nothing I know about, as I keep saying."

"A story," Heimrich said. "Or, a place to put a bite."

Felson sighed. He said, "How many times

do I have to say it?"

"Shakedown," Heimrich said. "Blackmail."

Felson made a sound of deprecation with tongue and teeth. It came through fat lips. He said, "Think of that, now."

"I've heard," Heimrich said, "that you do, Felson."

Felson made the sound again. He said he couldn't help what Heimrich heard. He said, "*Shakeup!* is dedicated to the exposure of corruption and immorality. Published to improve the moral tone of the community."

"Unquote," Heimrich said.

Felson sighed again. He said that Heimrich was beginning to bore him. He said that if Heimrich thought he could do anything about anything he could always try. He said, "I don't know a damn thing about what Beale was doing up there in the sticks."

"All right," Heimrich said. "What do you know about Beale?"

"He worked for me. Reporter out on the West Coast. Brought along a tip he thought we might like. Pretty juic— a suggestion of quite deplorable behavior by a star whose name to many misguided movie-goers had become —"

"Unquote," Heimrich said. "And bought a job with his tip. Anything else you know?"

"We make it a policy," Felson said, "not

to probe into the pasts of our employees."

"I'll bet," Heimrich said. "How old was he? Or didn't you probe into that, either?"

"Thirty," Felson said. "According to his social security record."

Felson put fat hands on the arms of the fat chair and began to lift himself. He came out of the chair with less effort than Heimrich had supposed would be needed. He was a man of rubber, with some of rubber's resilience. When he was on his feet, he said, "Sorry you've got to rush off."

"Sometime," Heimrich said, "there'll be a squeal. Sometime they'll catch you at it, Mr. Felson."

"Unquote," Felson said. "Meanwhile, the word is scram."

Heimrich considered briefly. He decided that that probably was the word.

In his car, Heimrich again considered. There did not seem to be anything further to be done immediately. He looked at his watch, found that it was only eleven-fifteen — earlier than he would have thought. Tuck in one loose end, perhaps, and round off the day.

He drove a few blocks and found a telephone, and looked up a number and dialed. He was informed, after a pause, that he was connected with the Men's Faculty Club of

Dyckman University. He asked whether Professor Walter Brinkley was still at the club.

The club was afraid not; the club would check. Heimrich waited. Professor Brinkley had just left.

The loose end, therefore, left to dangle. Heimrich drove up parkways in the warm night to Van Brunt Center and the Old Stone Inn, and checked in from there, and learned there was nothing from North Wellwood that wouldn't keep, and that Forniss was staying there, in the Maples Inn. Heimrich thought of calling him and looked at his watch and found it was no longer earlier than he had thought.

Wrap it up until morning, Heimrich thought. Call it a day. He called it one.

As such things go, Walter Brinkley thought, this one had gone at least as well as could be expected. Professor Francis Anderson (dear old Andy) had been duly welcomed to the rather sere pasture of the superannuated. Professor Anderson had taken it well, with grace and with somewhat fewer clichés than Brinkley had (secretly, of course) anticipated. And his own performance, Walter Brinkley concluded — driving the M.G. with confidence and in excess of the speed limit on the Saw Mill River Parkway — had been acceptable. He had been brief in introductions, at any rate, and one or two of the things he had said struck him, in retrospect, as rather good. Not too good, of course — it would have been inappropriate to be too good. One sought, in such surroundings, under such gently melancholy circumstances, the chuckle, not the belly laugh.

The food had, of course, been execrable. And, after dinner, capping his night in the lounge, Professor Abel Milner had grown doleful — as a man with wife and children, on an associate professor's salary may well — and had fallen to saying, "Why?" in the saddest of tones, adding from time to time that that was what he asked himself. But he had been much more cheerful by the time Walter dropped him at his apartment near Riverside and Walter's own somewhat lowered spirits — it had to be admitted that "Why?" was a question one was likely to ask oneself at intervals — climbed pleasantly. The M.G. was really on its best behavior and the night was fine.

And, of course, the burr no longer rankled in his mind — had, at any rate, been isolated and identified and waited only to be passed on. Tomorrow, with suitable apologies for proffering so small a gift, he would hand it to Heimrich. It had been a little foolish to take it, and himself, so seriously as he had earlier, when he had tried to reach Heimrich on the telephone. If anything would keep, a thing so tiny — a guess at the best — certainly would.

Brinkley paused for the lights at the northern end of the Saw Mill River and, permitted, drove on. He followed familiar roads to North Wellwood. He traversed Hayride Lane to his own driveway and went up it and got out of the M.G. and opened the garage door, and got back into the M.G. and drove it in, and got out of it and closed the garage door. It was then, as he stood still facing the door, that the night was filled with a great roaring noise. Simultaneously, there were several sharp cracking sounds in the wood of the door beside him and several sharp stinging pains in his buttocks. And, simultaneously with these things, Walter Brinkley threw himself to the side, felt himself falling and — falling, in a final instant — heard the angry blasting sound again and knew that the second barrel of a shotgun had been fired.

It was as if the sound had shaken out all the lights. Walter Brinkley fell into darkness.

The telephone by Heimrich's bed rang once. By its second ring Heimrich, who had been deep in sleep, had it and he said,

"Heimrich," and, after an instant, "Yes, Charlie?"

"The professor's been shot," Sergeant Forniss said, from North Wellwood. "Shotgun again. Outside his garage. His man just called."

Heimrich swore briefly. He said, "Killed?"

"No," Forniss said. "The man says not. I'm on my way now. Ambulance is too. But — alive, the man says. You'll —"

"Fast as I can," Heimrich said.

The act of murder fills Captain Heimrich with deep and bitter anger — an emotion below the surface, below any professional attitude. He had felt that bitter anger when he looked at the torn body of Caroline Wilkins and again — although he had no reason to think well of a man who was probably up to something nasty — when he saw the similarly shattered body of Conrad Beale. And now again — but this time the anger surged more hotly. Brinkley was a man he knew, liked. And Brinkley was a man who had been trying to tell him something.

And I, Heimrich thought, called it a day and went to bed. The bitterness, then, was married to self-contempt.

# XII

A good many lights were on on the lower floor of Walter Brinkley's house, and a good many cars were in the drive and turnaround. Flashlights bobbed and quested on the lawns, among the shrubs. None of this, Sergeant Forniss told Heimrich, was bothering the professor. The professor was out.

"Not from being shot," Forniss said. "A few pellets, mostly where you'd expect. Seat of the pants. But, when he fell, he banged his head. On a sundial, of all things."

Heimrich waited.

"Concussion, the doctor says," Forniss told him. "Got him upstairs. Doesn't want to move him for a while. Then they'll take him to the hospital and do x-rays."

"He'll make it?"

"Yep. Anyway, the doctor's pretty sure. Just concussion. No sign of a fracture. In a way, he got a break. Whoever had the gun figured, when Brinkley fell, that he'd got Brinkley. And then — got going. Washington was there in a couple of minutes. Quite a guy, Harry Washington. Because, how did he know the gun hadn't been reloaded? Plenty of time for that before he could get down."

"Harry's quite a guy," Heimrich agreed. "I suppose he didn't see anything?"

They were in the living room of Walter Brinkley's pleasant house. As if he had heard his name, Harry Washington came into the room through a door at the rear. He wore a white coat. He carried a silver tray with cups on it, and a silver coffeepot. He put the tray down on a table.

"I thought you might both like some coffee," Harry said. He was no longer, in inflection, in attitude, an old Southern retainer. He was a man who thought a couple of other men, working late at night, might like coffee to sustain them.

They had coffee.

"Sit down, Harry," Heimrich, said. "Have some yourself."

Harry Washington smiled faintly, and sat down. "I've had all the coffee I can take right now," he said. "What would anybody have against Mr. Brinkley, captain?"

Heimrich didn't know, and said so. He said, "I suppose you didn't see anything?"

Harry Washington took a packet of cigarettes from the pocket of the white jacket, and lighted a cigarette.

"No," he said. "Only heard. A shotgun, twice. Both barrels close together. That was at twelve-thirty-five, give or take a minute or so."

"Good," Heimrich said. "That you looked, I mean. You were asleep?"

He had been in his room, Harry said. Not really asleep. He was not supposed to wait up for the professor; nevertheless, he usually did.

"But apparently I dropped off," Harry said. "The gun waked me up. I was pretty sure Mr. Brinkley hadn't come in. I'd have heard him." He drew deeply on the cigarette. "The stairs creak," Harry said.

He moved when he heard the shots; moved fast. His way downstairs took him past Brinkley's bedroom. The door was open, a night light burning, the room empty. He ran down the stairs and turned on the outside floodlight as he passed the switch.

The professor was lying near the garage door. Harry thought he was dead. He found that he wasn't, but was breathing with, Harry thought, a good deal of effort. It was evident that, whatever else had happened to him, he had hit his head violently against the sundial as he fell.

"I carried him inside," Harry said. "Perhaps I shouldn't have moved him but —" He shrugged his shoulders. "The doctor says it didn't do any harm," he said.

He had telephoned the State Police for an ambulance; had telephoned a doctor down the road; had, then, telephoned Sergeant Forniss at the inn. He had put blankets over the unconscious man and, with a damp cloth, staunched the blood from the head wound. Brinkley had not been bleeding much.

"The doctor got here first," Harry said. "Then the ambulance. The doctor says he'll be all right." He drew again on the cigarette; ground it out. "What would anybody have against a man like Mr. Brinkley?" he said. "A good man."

"I don't know," Heimrich said. "We'll find out. You didn't hear anybody? Running, say? Or driving off in a car?"

"No," Harry said. "Probably he — whoever it was — got startled when he saw Mr. Brinkley fall. I was still inside then — running down the stairs. Making some noise myself. No, I didn't hear anything."

"He might have been waiting," Heimrich said. "Might have had time to reload and wait."

"Well," Harry Washington said, "there wasn't any point in worrying about that, captain. And — there wasn't time."

Harry sat for a moment. Then he got up and refilled Heimrich's cup, and Forniss's. The coffee was very good.

"He may be out for hours, the doctor says," Harry told them. "But — I'd doubt he saw anything. From the way he was lying, I'd guess he had just pulled the door down, was still standing in front of it, when this bastard —" He stopped with that.

Heimrich finished his coffee. "Let's go look," he said, and the three went out, across the terrace, to the garage turnaround, where the floodlight beat down whitely on gravel.

The sundial was a few feet from the corner of the garage — more ornament, Heimrich thought, than teller of the passing hours. There was a little blood on the edge of the stone plate. "Right here, he was," Harry Washington said, and showed them. Brinkley had, it was evident, staggered several paces before he fell. It was probable, Heimrich thought, that he had tripped on the coping of the driveway.

The wooden garage door was scarred, where shot had hit it. The pellets had not, however, penetrated deeply.

Bushes were planted around the curving edge of the turnaround. Any one of them would have provided concealment. The nearest was some thirty feet distant from the door. At a guess, whoever had tried to kill Walter Brinkley, had fired over, or through, one of the bushes. The shot had had time to scatter,

233

the aim had been a little to one side. And so Brinkley was still alive. Two troopers with flashlights were behind the bushes, searching. It seemed unlikely they would find much. The ground was hard.

They went back inside and waited.

"You showed a picture of Beale around, Charlie?" Heimrich asked, while they waited. "Or didn't you get it soon enough?"

Thanks to somebody's Polaroid, Forniss had got a quick photograph of Conrad Beale.

"He looked dead," Forniss said. "But the face was clear enough."

Admiral Bennett — stiff as ever, crisp as ever, but with a look of almost final fatigue on his face — had looked at the picture; looked at it for several seconds.

"Yes," he said. "That's the man. Older, of course. Looks more like a rat than ever. But that's Beale."

Commander Wilkins had looked at the photograph with stony eyes. He, too, had looked at it a long time, and then he had shaken his head. "I never saw him," Wilkins said, and handed the photograph back.

"He didn't show anything," Forniss said. "Could be he's telling the truth. Could be he isn't. By the way — he says he left the undertaker's sometime after seven. He doesn't know when. But — he didn't get back to the house until almost ten. Says he was just driving around. You can drive quite a ways in that time."

"Yes," Heimrich said. "Of course — he probably didn't want to see anybody right away. He's taken quite a beating, Charlie. She was young, Charlie. Very lovely. Before —"

"She gets killed," Forniss said, "while her first husband is in the neighborhood. And nobody'll say where her present husband was — including him. And then, her first husband gets killed. And her second husband is — driving around somewhere. Doesn't remember where — just driving. And, it's a hundred to one the gun was his gun."

"Now Charlie," Heimrich said. "I don't say it couldn't have been that way."

"They might have thought he was safely somewhere else," Forniss said. "He might have meant them to."

"Yes," Heimrich said. "The others?"

Neither Alan Kelley nor Dorcas Cameron had seen Beale alive, if the man photographed dead was Beale. Or — neither admitted it. Dorcas had said, "But why would the old man —" and stopped with that because, Forniss said, Alan Kelley had pressed her arm.

"She can't get away from it," Forniss said. "Or — that's the idea she gives."

Forniss has, Heimrich thought, precisely

the right attitude for a cop to have: Don't believe anything until you have to.

"She and Kelley were getting a marriage license in New York," he said, mildly. "You get around to Mrs. Craig?"

Forniss had got around to both the Craigs. He had driven up the drive to the monstrous house only after he had made sure lights were on in it; he had found Mrs. Craig — but not, especially, Craig himself — co-operative, but not helpful.

"He started out scratchy," Forniss said. "What the hell was a cop doing bothering *him?* That sort of thing. She quieted him down. He'd never seen the man before. She hadn't either — and it wasn't the man who had tried to sell her brushes. The same type, perhaps, but not at all the same man."

"You believed them?"

Forniss hesitated but primarily, Heimrich thought, because he was loath to believe anyone. He compromised, finally. He said he didn't disbelieve them.

"I —" he began, and Harry Washington, who had taken the coffee tray out, came back. He said there was something he had forgotten to tell them — something that probably didn't matter, but that they'd probably want to hear about. At a little after ten o'clock, somebody called the professor on the telephone. Harry had said the professor wasn't there.

"Man or woman?" Heimrich asked.

Harry shook his head.

In a sense, it had been neither. Actually, of course, a woman. But — a telephone operator, with a person-to-person call. "New York," in the abstract apparently, was calling Professor Walter Brinkley, and only him.

"I said the professor was in New York," Harry told them. "That he wouldn't be back, probably, until after midnight. She said, 'Thank you,' and hung up."

"You've no idea who —" Heimrich said, and stopped, because the question was meaningless. The telephone company doesn't tell who.

"No," Harry said. "I thought possibly it was you calling again, captain. From New York."

Heimrich shook his head. But he was reminded of another question — probably also fruitless. Had Harry any idea what it was Brinkley had wanted to tell the police?

"No," Harry said.

"Yesterday around noon —" Heimrich said, and looked at his watch. It was Thursday, now; had been Thursday for some time. "Tuesday," he said. "When Mrs. Wilkins probably was killed. You and Mr. Brinkley were in the village?"

They had been. They had left the house about eleven-thirty, in the station wagon — Harry to market; Brinkley to go to the library. They had got back a little before one o'clock.

"There weren't any shots before we left," Harry said. "None after we got back. But, you'd already decided it happened sometime around noon."

"During the morning," Heimrich said, "what was Mr. Brinkley doing?"

"Working," Harry said. "Typewriter going pretty steadily — from around nine until — oh, eleven-fifteen."

Heimrich briefly closed his eyes. He opened them. He wondered whether, without disturbing Mr. Brinkley, he could see the room Brinkley worked in — the study, he supposed it was.

"Office, we call it," Harry said. "Yes. I don't think we'll bother him. Other side of the house from his bedroom."

Heimrich and Harry Washington went up the wooden stairs as silently as they could. The "office" was a square room; it held a desk and a typewriter on a separate table. It held a good deal of manuscript, neatly piled. Sitting at the typewriter, with a window behind him, Brinkley faced another window. Raising his eyes from the typewriter, as it was to be assumed he sometimes did — on the chance the word he sought was flying by outside — Brinkley looked up the ridge. He looked, Heimrich discovered — by sitting in the chair in front of the typewriter — over meadowland toward the old Adams house. The light was milky now, from half a moon. But in daylight, probably, a man with good eyes, if he happened to be looking at the right time, might well see, and identify, callers who walked from parked cars to the front door of the square white house.

"Mr. Brinkley see well, Harry?" Heimrich asked.

"For a man his age, very well," Harry said. "At a distance, especially." Harry stood and looked through the window, up the ridge. "Only," he said, "we weren't here at the time, captain."

"Someone might have come earlier," Heimrich said. "Been there for some little time before — acting. Nobody's come forward to say he was, Harry."

"It would explain a good deal," Harry said. "I see that, captain. If Mr. Brinkley saw someone. Didn't realize what he had seen was important until later. And — the wrong person found out he'd been seen."

Heimrich sat at the typewriter for a moment longer, looking up the ridge through the milky night. There were no lights on at the Adams house; not on this side of the house, at any rate. Probably, what the professor had to tell about was something he had seen, sitting in this chair, looking through this window — but looking, as Heimrich did not, over sunlit fields. Found significance in what he had seen — when? When he had seen the same person again, under other circumstances?

There was little point in sitting there, wondering vaguely. Possibly, without meaning to, Professor Walter Brinkley had somehow become in some sense the catalytic agent Heimrich so often finds in the complex of a crime. Obviously, not precisely that. The professor had been acted upon.

They went out into the upstairs hall. A door opened on the other side of the hall and a man came out through it, carrying an identifying bag. He did not close the door immediately and, looking into the room, Heimrich could see Walter Brinkley, propped up in bed. In the dim light in the room, Brinkley appeared to be sleeping peacefully, and looked healthily pink of face. The pinkness was accentuated by the wide white bandage the professor was wearing.

"The police, doctor," Heimrich said. "How's the professor?"

"Concussed," the doctor said. "Rather mildly, I think. No sign of a fracture. Wake up with a headache, probably. And, won't be comfortable sitting down for a few days."

"He'll remember what happened?"

"I can't tell you that," the doctor said. "Probably not at once. But perhaps he will. Concussion does odd things sometimes."

"How long?"

"Before he comes to? I can't tell you that, either. He's had some sedation — not a great deal. He might come out of it in a couple of hours. It might be — oh, twenty-four. I've got a nurse coming."

He waited.

"I'll leave a man here," Heimrich said. "Just to be sure."

"When he comes out of it," the doctor said, "I don't want him questioned until I've had another look at him. That's understood?"

"Now doctor," Heimrich said. "Naturally."

"He's going to be all right, doctor?" Harry said, and there was anxiety in his voice, in his dark, intelligent and friendly face.

"Don't you worry, Harry," the doctor said.

Heimrich and Harry Washington went downstairs. The doctor went back into Brinkley's room. Forniss was no longer in the living room. Heimrich looked out through the french doors. Forniss was in the floodlighted area in front of the garage. He was talking to a trooper, who was holding something. I'll be damned, Heimrich thought, and went out to join Forniss and the trooper, who was holding a shotgun by a cord run through the trigger guard.

There had been no real effort, apparently, to hide the shotgun, both barrels of which had been fired. It was lying, partly under bushes, some twenty feet beyond the row of shrubbery which circled the turnaround. A person taking the quickest way — the quickest inconspicuous way — toward the road might have dropped it there.

"It looks," Forniss said, "as if our friend has decided to call it a day."

Heimrich looked at the gun without touching it. A good gun, a sleek gun. Fourteen gauge. A new gun, apparently. A gun, presumably, which had killed twice and been aimed to kill again. And then, tossed casually aside, to be found by who ever chanced to stumble on it.

And this, Heimrich thought, did not make any sense at all. North Wellwood is in reservoir country. It is childishly easy, thereabouts, to dispose of any object of moderate size by taking it to the nearest reservoir and throwing it into deep water. If the murderer was done with the gun — because he had run out of subjects? because he had decided to change methods? — why not drown it in deep water? The answer was evident — he wanted it found.

Presumably, it would turn out to be the gun from the Wilkins house, could be identified as that. Then — discarded to tie back to someone there? Or — by the very obviousness of the method chosen, to exonerate the most likely?

"Never thought we'd see this one," Forniss said, putting a finger on it. "Why?"

"Now Charlie," Heimrich said, and continued to wonder why.

"One thing's sure," Forniss said. "There won't be prints. It won't be that easy. Gloves, unless it's been wiped."

"I don't suppose so," Heimrich said. "Take it along in, Drury. Have the boys go over it."

Drury went off to one of the police cars, the gun dangling from the cord through its trigger guard.

A small car came up the drive. A middle-aged woman, who wore a light coat over a white uniform, got out of it. The nurse had arrived.

"Now?" Forniss said.

Now they left somebody — somebody who would stay awake — and got what sleep they could. (Heimrich hoped that, this time, it would be safe to call it a day.) Tomorrow — but not really tomorrow; really later today — they would get on with it.

"Anything in town?" Forniss said as, with a trooper posted, they went toward a car.

Heimrich told him, as they drove to the Maples Inn, what there had been in town.

"It doesn't tie in too well, does it?" Forniss said, being told. "Looks like Dutch and his little orphan Opal are out of it. Just one of those things that bob up."

"Probably," Heimrich said. "What brought Beale here, then?"

"Came to see the lady," Forniss said. "Maybe — had some business with her? Something phony about the divorce, maybe? Or maybe — just wanted to see the lady. And the commander found them together and misunderstood. Or — *didn't* misunderstand. Got her first and Beale got away. But, didn't get away far enough, or fast enough."

"And the professor?"

"Saw the commander when he drove up. Could even have seen him go around back of the house with the gun."

"Now Charlie," Heimrich said. "Brinkley wouldn't have called that something 'not important.' He told Lieutenant Kelley it wasn't."

He didn't, Forniss said, argue that there weren't things to check out. But, after all, Commander Wilkins certainly had a habit of not being where you could put a finger on him.

"Like a cricket," Forniss amplified, taking Heimrich up with him to share a room at the inn for what little of the night remained.

# XIII

Walter Brinkley's first thought on awakening was that he had seldom had so deep and restful a sleep and his second, somewhat confusingly unrelated, that it was still some days from the Fourth of July. Then why, Brinkley wondered, so large a firecracker, fired so close under his bedroom window? Particularly since it was years since anybody had set off a firecracker in the neighborhood, except, of course, at the country club's annual celebration.

It must be, Brinkley decided, around nine o'clock or possibly even later. The curtains, drawn across the wide window of his bedroom, did not quite meet, and the shaft of light which came between them — it was another bright day, which was pleasant — struck the mirror in the closet door. This gave him, if a little roughly, an idea what time it was. Better than the sundial by the garage, which had, unfortunately, no sun to dial until shortly before noon. (Why had he thought of the sundial?)

And why, for that matter, had he gone to bed wearing a hat? He could feel it pressing, not unpleasantly but inexplicably, around his head. Yet there was no question that he was in bed — his own bed, and comfortable in it. Why, then — He reached up and touched the hat, which did, now he thought of it, seem a little tight. It was there, certainly. The Misses Monroe must think it rather odd of him to wear so tight a hat while taking them to lunch. The Misses Monroe —

And then it came to him, devastatingly — came like another explosion in his mind. Here he was, lying comfortably in bed (to which he had worn a hat) and there was a thing of vital importance which he should have done hours ago. He had, with that realization, a sinking of the spirits such as he could not recall having had before in all of his life. When Grace had died there had been a sinking — deeper, a sinking into hopeless sadness, into defeat — but that had been different in quality. This was more nearly a sense of guilt. (In whom, just recently, had he watched, in sympathy, while such a guilt sense grew?) There was this thing which he should have done long ago and had not done. (Why had he not? Had he merely forgotten? Was it, inexcusably, something which had slipped from a fuzzy mind?)

There would, Brinkley realized, be time for that later — self-recrimination, while justified, while all very well, would now amount to self-indulgence. Now, late as it was, he must try to make amends. And he must begin the try immediately.

Brinkley swung his legs out of bed and stood up. Unexpectedly, the movement resulted in some dizziness, and this puzzled him, because he was never dizzy. A sign of age, of course — perhaps a precursor of something. But there was no time for that, either. When he had rectified his failure — his really vital failure — there would be time, along with self-recrimination, to indulge in self-pity. Not now.

The dizziness passed. Probably not, then, really a warning of anything more dire to follow. He had merely got up too quickly. Might happen to anybody. Get dressed and —

Walter Brinkley pulled the curtains apart. A really beautiful day. No time to stand, in pajamas, in front of a wide window and admire a beautiful day. Get dressed and —

Walter turned quickly and found he was facing himself in the mirror of the closet door. Facing, more exactly, two of himself, partially super-imposed. Two semi-detached Walter Brinkleys, wearing white hats. *White* hats? He had never worn a white hat in his life. He would take it off at —

He reached up to remove the hat and then remembered that he had been strictly enjoined *not* to take the hat off. Someone in authority had said, "Now you must leave that alone, professor." Harry? It did not sound quite like Harry. He could not think who else it might have been and decided that that, too, was a thing which would have to be left for later. The point now was to get out of the house and away without letting Harry — the dear, solicitous man! — stop him. Harry would not let him go without breakfast. Harry would be at his most retainerly — was that a word? — and would say, "No suh, professor, not less you has your breakfuss first, suh." Perhaps even "not less'n" if the mood was really on him. Circumvent Harry, therefore. Explain it to him later — say that what had to be done had been of dominant importance, nothing which could wait even on Harry's scrambled eggs. What a way he has with scrambled eggs, Walter thought, a shade wistfully, and was at the same time pleased to notice that the two Walter Brinkleys had merged into one. (Still wearing a white hat, to be sure.) The thing to do was to move about very quietly, so that Harry would not hear him.

Walter opened the closet door and found slacks and put them on over his pajamas. He put tennis shoes on bare feet — tennis shoes make very little noise. Harry must not hear him go down the stairs and out across the terrace to the garage. It would be difficult to open the garage door quietly. Probably the best thing to do would be not to try to be quiet then — he would have to chance it then; slam the door up and get going fast. The station wagon then — it faced out. When he had come back from talking with the Misses Monroe — what they must have thought of his wearing so peculiar a hat! — he had not bothered to back the M.G. in, but had run it in straight ahead. To take the M.G., although certainly it was much faster, would mean backing out and circling around, and by then Harry would be on him.

He looked at himself — only one of himself still — in the door mirror. (It was certainly the strangest hat he had ever seen. When ever, *why* ever, had he bought a hat like that?) The pajama jacket was a bright yellow, with a black collar and black piping on the pocket. (What was one supposed to carry in a pajama pocket? Then, why a pocket at all? He relentlessly pulled his mind back from its tendency to dither. He would have to do something about his mind. Later.) He could hardly go out — go where he was going, especially, in a bright yellow pajama jacket with black accents. Particularly, he thought, *black* accents. (Don't dither, professor!) He put on a tweed jacket over the pajama top. Much better.

One thing remained. Where was it? On the top shelf of the closet. He was quite sure it was there, and stood on tiptoe and could just reach the top shelf. Not — yes, here it was.

Walter Brinkley removed the protective wrapping — a felt bag which had originally swathed a silver coffeepot — from a .32 caliber revolver. He put the revolver in the right hand pocket of his jacket and the permit to possess it, which had been in the bag too, in the left hand pocket. He went to the bedroom door and listened for several moments and did not hear Harry stirring. Probably out in the kitchen, getting things together for breakfast making.

Walter opened the door very slowly and carefully, so it would not squeak. He went out into the corridor and to the stairs and, on the stairs, very carefully down next the railing, because he had heard that, trodden on so rather than in the center, stairs tended to protest less.

He found the front door open, and opened the screen as carefully as he had the bedroom door, and then went the long way around the house, because Harry might be setting the breakfast table up on the terrace, since it was such a fine morning.

He still had the dash across the open area

of the turnaround, the yanking up of the door — the time of speed, not of caution. With any luck, he would get away with it. . . .

It was not, actually, anybody's fault that Walter Brinkley did get away with it. Trooper Townsend was stationed at the house not to prevent the escape of any of its inmates — nobody had supposed that any of its inmates would desire escape — but to stop anybody who tried to come in with the intention of doing Professor Brinkley further harm. There was, therefore, no reason why he should not have gone to the kitchen to make himself some coffee, as Harry Washington had suggested he might want to do, and for the doing of which Harry had provided.

And it was not, to Bernadine Piper, R.N., as if the patient's condition were at all critical. He was only a little concussed, and sleeping naturally, and probably would sleep naturally for hours. Breathing regular, pulse normal, everything in order. The patient might be a little nervous on regaining consciousness and need to be reassured — that was, she was quite certain, the only actual duty she would have, and that not for hours. Of course, if the condition changed — that was really what doctor wanted her there for. Well, it wasn't going to. Not in the time it would take her to go downstairs and make herself a cup of coffee.

Harry Washington had decided that he would be no good to the professor when the professor needed him if he was dead for sleep. He had therefore, quite sensibly, gone to get sleep. He slept late.

"Good morning, officer," Nurse Piper said to Trooper Townsend in the pleasant kitchen of the Brinkley house. "Two minds with but a single thought, I see."

It was very well put, Trooper Townsend thought, and he said, "Good morning, nurse. It looks like another fine day."

"Let *me* do that, officer," Nurse Piper said, and took the tea kettle from him and continued to pour boiling water into the cone of filter paper. "Doesn't it smell wonderful?"

"It sure —"

Trooper Townsend stopped on that. The banging sound of a garage door lifted violently, slapping against the bumpers at track end, was loud through the open window. Trooper Townsend jumped to the window and looked toward the garage.

A station wagon leaped out of the garage. A plumpish man in his late middle years was at the wheel. He wore a white bandage around his head. He had the car going at quite a dangerous speed down the driveway.

"Damn," Trooper Townsend said, watching the departure of Professor Walter Brink-ley.

"Oh dear," Nurse Piper said. "What will *doctor* say?"

There is no use asking men trained as experts if they really mean what they say, have really found what they report having found. Captain M. L. Heimrich did not, therefore, ask the fingerprint man if he was sure — really sure — that he had found the almost perfect prints of a man's four fingers and his thumb, together with that of part of the palm of his hand, on the barrel of a shotgun. If he said he had, he had. It was not his problem to explain them. There they were.

A man's right hand. On the gun not where a hand would have been held while the gun was fired. Where a man might pick up a gun to carry it. That was obvious.

There were prints there and only there. None on the stock, none on trigger or trigger guard. None anywhere else on the sleek weapon.

"Wiped off?" Heimrich asked, sitting in the parlor of the Maples Inn — and an odd place it was for such a report to be proffered, be received — looking at the gun and the man who held it.

"Probably. Except there."

Which, obviously, made no sense. Or, more precisely, made only the sense of almost unbelievable carelessness. To use a gun in an effort to kill — actually to kill, in all probability; but that could not yet be proved — then to throw the gun away with a perfect set of fingerprints on it. To wipe off all the gun —

"The shells?" Heimrich said. While putting shells into a gun one often leaves prints on them.

"Clean," the fingerprint man said.

"You've lifted them? Made photographs?"

The fingerprint man looked as weary as a sergeant may permit himself to look when a captain asks silly questions. Heimrich smiled and said he was sorry.

It had been, then, a little after eight. Heimrich and Forniss had breakfasted. Forniss had driven the car to a filling station for gas. He had come into the parlor and heard what the fingerprint man had found. Forniss said he would be damned, and looked at the gun with some reproach. But he brightened.

"Nice of somebody," he said. "Puts it in our laps, doesn't it. Not the kind of thing you expect."

"No," Heimrich said. "It isn't, Charlie. Go to a lot of trouble and somebody puts it in our laps."

The captain, Charles Forniss thought, seems a little disappointed. Can't say I blame him but —

"All we've got to do," Forniss said, "is to get us some nice prints to go with them."

"Yes," Heimrich said. "That's all, naturally." He held a hand out and the fingerprint man put a glossy photograph of fingerprints into it. They were very nice prints indeed; Heimrich doubted whether he and Sergeant Forniss, collecting as now they would have to collect, would come up with any quite so clear. But — they would get them clear enough.

"Old Ash Adams," Heimrich said. "His son, while you're about it. Joe Parks. The professor, I suppose. Although I doubt he shot at himself. Harry Washington's, naturally."

Forniss raised his eyebrows at that.

"No," Heimrich said. "I don't, Charlie. Just thorough investigation of all possibilities, as it says in the book."

"You'll do the others?"

"Yes," Heimrich said. "I'll do the others." He paused. "Couldn't have been a woman?" he asked the fingerprint man, in spite of himself. The sergeant, this time, allowed himself the semblance of a sigh. He said, very carefully, "No, captain. Not any woman I've ever seen."

Forniss took a copy of the photograph from the fingerprint man. He said, "I don't envy you with the admiral."

Heimrich did not envy himself.

They got up; they started toward the parlor door, Heimrich in the lead. Mrs. Lambert appeared, and occupied the doorway. Mrs. Lambert was comfortable, as an innkeeper should be.

"Isn't it a beautiful morning?" Mrs. Lambert asked them. "But so dreadful about the poor professor!"

Heimrich has long since ceased to be amazed by the speed with which, in rural communities, news travels. He is now only, with each new example, mildly surprised. He agreed that it was dreadful about the professor, but that the doctor seemed to feel —

"I know," Mrs. Lambert said. "That's such good news. But coming right on top of poor Mr. Beale and that dreadful, *dreadful* thing about the commander's wife." Suddenly, as if all these things had only in that instant become real, Mrs. Lambert's comfortable face fell into lines of discomfort, of unhappiness. *"Here,"* she said, in disbelief. "Here in North Wellwood!" Then, for the first time, she noticed that Captain Heimrich was carrying a shotgun. Her eyes widened at that. She said, "My *good*ness" and then, looking up from the gun to the man carrying it, "Is that —"

"We don't know," Heimrich said. "But — almost certainly the gun that was fired at Mr. Brinkley. You don't recognize it?"

He asked that, because she looked as if she did. But she said, "Goodness no. One gun is just like any other to me." And then, "But I mustn't keep you." She stepped aside.

They started again. They had gone from parlor door to front door when, behind them, Mrs. Lambert said, "*Oh*. Captain."

They stopped. "Go ahead," Heimrich said to Sergeant Forniss, and Forniss went ahead while Heimrich turned back.

"I came to tell you something," Mrs. Lambert said. "And almost forgot what I came for. Isn't that ridiculous?"

Heimrich smiled and waited.

"But probably you already know about it," she said. "Probably the commander told you himself?"

"No," Heimrich said. "At least — told me what, Mrs. Lambert?"

"About coming here to see Mr. Beale," she said. "Not finding him, of course, because Mr. Beale — the poor man — wasn't here. I don't suppose it means anything but — I didn't know the commander even *knew* Mr. Beale. The poor man."

"No," Heimrich said. "I didn't either. Let's —"

He took Mrs. Lambert's comfortable arm gently and led her back into the parlor. He said, "Now Mrs. Lambert. Tell me about it."

"I only just heard myself," she said. "When William came on this morning. William's the bartender, you know."

Heimrich nodded.

"About eight o'clock last evening," Mrs. Lambert said. "While you and the sergeant were having dinner in the dining room. He didn't really ask William, but William got just a glimpse and he's quite sure. He —"

A tall straight man, black-haired — the man William, who could see from behind the bar, diagonally through a door, was sure had been Commander Brady Wilkins — had come into the small lobby of the Maples Inn at about eight o'clock the evening before. He had asked a passing waiter if a Mr. Beale was staying there — a Mr. Conrad Beale.

The waiter, who was going from dining room, across lobby, toward taproom with an order, and who was in a hurry, had said he didn't know, he was sure. "An extra waiter," Mrs. Lambert said. "All these newspaper people, you know." The waiter had suggested that Commander Wilkins — if it was Commander Wilkins — use the house phone, and showed

259

him where it was. And some man had used it. Molly remembered that.

"My youngest daughter, you know," Mrs. Lambert said. "On the switchboard sometimes."

A man had used the house telephone at about that hour. From the switchboard, Molly Lambert could not see him. He had asked if a Mr. Conrad Beale was staying at the hotel and Molly had checked and said yes, in room twelve in the annex, and should she ring him? Told to ring him, she had, and had got no answer. She was sorry. Mr. Beale did not seem to be in his room. Perhaps the dining room? The caller might look in there.

But it did not appear that the caller had looked in there. Nobody had seen him, or remembered seeing him.

"You were facing the door, as I recall it," Mrs. Lambert said. "You didn't see him, did you?"

Captain Heimrich had not seen the commander. He imagined that, if Commander Wilkins had looked in the dining room — stood in the doorway, looked around the room for Conrad Beale — he would have seen him.

"So," Mrs. Lambert said, "he must have just gone out and, I suppose, gone home. The poor, *poor* man. Such a dreadful thing to come home to."

"Yes," Heimrich said. "A very dreadful thing. Mrs. Lambert — somebody could go from outside into the annex without being seen?"

Heimrich knew the answer as he finished the question. Somebody — anybody — easily could have. The two buildings were detached; there was no lobby in the annex.

"Unless a maid happened to be there," Mrs. Lambert said. "Or one of the guests, of course. Captain Heimrich — you don't *think?*"

"Mr. Beale's room was broken into," Heimrich said. "I don't know when. Some time before you gave the passkey to Sergeant Forniss. And —"

"*Broken* into," Mrs. Lambert said. "*Broken?* And nobody *told* me! The help one gets nowadays! The — yes, what is it, Daisy?"

Daisy was an angular woman in white, with an expression of the utmost trepidation. She trembled in the doorway.

"Miz Lambert," she said. "*The door-of-room-twelve-is-all-broke.* I left it to last because Mr. Beale — And somebody broke in. And —"

"All right, Daisy," Mrs. Lambert said. "You can't help it. There's a checkout in fifteen."

"Oh, Miz Lambert, thank you," Daisy said, and trembled out of the doorway.

"Odd numbers in the main building," Mrs. Lambert said. "Even in the annex." She said this mechanically. She said, "*Captain!* You don't think the *commander* — But — he's a *Navy* officer."

"Now Mrs. Lambert," Heimrich said. "I don't know, naturally."

"The poor, poor man," she said. "Do you think — such a terrible shock, I mean — sometimes people such dreadful things happen to don't — don't really *know*."

"That's very true," Heimrich said, although he did not think that, in this instance, it would be likely to prove true. "And, of course, we don't know it was Commander Wilkins."

They didn't, of course. Driving from the inn to the Wilkins house Heimrich merely thought it very probable — very probable and very interesting. And he thought, also, that the most obvious things are always the most likely things — and that, perhaps, it was as well that Charlie Forniss was not a man given to saying "I told you so."

A man comes home unexpectedly — finds his wife with another man — a gun is handy and murder flares. But — one escapes. The man, in this case? Escapes, but is hunted down. Is lain in wait for — killed. The old thing, the obvious thing.

But — character must fit crime. Commander Wilkins was a man disciplined, a man matured. Such men do not grab guns up and kill with them, in jealous frenzy. The weaklings do such things, not the strong. Then —

But I, Heimrich thought, driving along Hayride Lane, past Professor Brinkley's house, have met Wilkins only once, and then briefly. I don't really know what kind of man he is; all I know is what he appears to be — a man controlled, holding himself tight. I am going only by the outside of the man.

# XIV

Sun was bright on the terrace of the old Adams house. Heimrich parked the police car on the turnaround and got out of it, carrying the shotgun. There was no point in guarding it from his fingers now; he had, duly photographed, duly attested, all the gun could tell him. He walked across the lawn toward the terrace and, still sitting — but sitting as if his arrival had frozen them in place — Dorcas Cameron and Alan Kelley watched him. Dorcas had a coffee cup halfway to her lips. For seconds she held it there. Then she put it down on a table and the tiny clink of the cup on metal was sharp in stillness.

They looked at Heimrich and they looked at the gun. Then Alan Kelley got up and took a step or two to the edge of the terrace. Both waited, without speaking, while Heimrich walked toward them, and up onto the terrace.

"So," Kelley said then, "you found it."

"Yes," Heimrich said. "At any rate — a gun. The right gun, Miss Cameron? The one from the hall closet?"

"I don't —" she said, and looked at the gun, apparently with care. "It could be," she said. "I don't know anything about guns." She looked at Heimrich. "Is it?" she said.

"Apparently," Heimrich told her, "it's the gun somebody used to shoot at the professor. Last night — early this morning."

But they would know about that. Everybody for a long way around would know about that.

"Captain," Dorcas said, "can't you stop — this? These dreadful things?"

"The professor will be all right," Heimrich said. But they would know that, too. They did know. Dorcas nodded.

She could not positively identify the gun. Perhaps Brady could. He had bought the gun. He knew about guns.

"Whoever it was shot at Brinkley," Kelley said. "He left the gun? Why?"

"Now lieutenant," Heimrich said. "Yes, he left it. I don't know why. Do you mind having your fingerprints taken?"

"Oh," Kelley said. "On the gun, I suppose?"

"It's a routine matter," Heimrich said, letting that be most of an answer. "For elimination."

"Of prints you've found?"

"Or might find," Heimrich said. "Well, lieutenant? Miss Cameron?"

"It doesn't matter," the girl said. She did

not look as quenched as she had looked the day before. Ash Adams, Heimrich thought, was fading out of her mind. He was also, Heimrich thought, fading out of the case. Adams had — again if his son was to be believed — been in his room, asleep, locked in, at twelve-thirty-five the night before. Now Dorcas Cameron's young face looked merely drawn, but with the beginning of lines in it — the tracings where time, finally, would leave lines. She looked as if she had slept little, for a long time.

Heimrich had brought an ink pad; he had brought slips of paper. He rolled the girl's fingers first, then Kelley's. He looked at the results, which were adequate. One of the boys might have done them better, but these were good enough. He took the photograph of the prints on the gun from his pocket and looked at it, and at both the new sets, and put slips and photograph back in his pocket. They looked at him. His eyes told them nothing.

"The admiral?" Heimrich said. "Commander Wilkins?"

The admiral answered his part of that. He answered it by coming up the path — the path from "the place." He came tall and erect, in slacks and a long-sleeved polo shirt. He nodded to Heimrich. He said, "Morning, Heimrich." He looked at the gun, which

Heimrich had put across the arms of a chair. "Nice piece," Admiral Bennett said. "That the one, Heimrich?"

Heimrich went through it again. He went through the part about prints again. It would have seemed impossible for the rigid admiral — was he always like that, Heimrich wondered? Or only now? — to stiffen further. He did. He also said, "Nonsense, man," in a tone of rebuke.

Heimrich should, he realized, shrivel. He did not. He said, "Yours. Everybody's, admiral."

"Oh," Bennett said and, as on the afternoon before, gray eyes met blue eyes, testing. "That way?" Bennett said.

"Yes," Heimrich said. "Naturally, admiral."

Briefly the admiral seemed to consider. But then, abruptly, he said, "Very well. Get on with it."

Heimrich got on with it. He compared the admiral's prints with those from the gun, and put both exhibits back in his pocket. When it became apparent Heimrich was not going to comment, Admiral Bennett said, "Well?"

To which Heimrich, at his blandest, said, "Now admiral." He was again looked at, but this time Heimrich briefly closed his eyes. At that, Admiral Bennett looked at his inky fingers.

"All right, Kelley," Admiral Bennett said, from the quarterdeck. "Get something."

"Sir," Kelley said and went into the house. He returned with a damp cloth and a dry one, and Heimrich waited patiently. When they had finished, he said, "Commander Wilkins around?"

"He just got to sleep, I think," Dorcas said. "After he came back last night — late — he went out around eleven to — just drive around, I think — be alone — after he came back I could hear him in — in their room — walking back and forth. It seemed like hours."

"Back late," Heimrich said. "About when, Miss Cameron?"

He could see realization come into her face; deepen in her face the lines traced there.

"No," she said. "You don't think —" But she stopped with that.

"The rest of you," Heimrich said. "You, admiral? Lieutenant?"

"I went to bed about eleven," Admiral Bennett said, his voice without inflection. "Slept, if you're interested. Always been able to sleep when the chance came."

After Wilkins had driven off, the admiral had gone up to the guest room, Dorcas and

Alan Kelley had sat on the terrace for, they both thought, about an hour. Sat talking. Then Kelley had made up a sofa bed in the living room and Dorcas had gone up to her room.

"None of you," Heimrich said, "heard shots? From the professor's house?"

"No," Admiral Bennett said, and Dorcas said, "No, captain." Kelley hesitated. He shrugged square shoulders. "Something waked me up," he said. "Partly waked me up. I don't know what time, or what it was. I went back to sleep. Only, the dream I had — the waking-up dream, if you know what I mean — was that a plane was shooting at us and all we had to answer with was a couple of obsolete five-inchers. Pretty hopeless, but we started to shoot and then I woke up. And felt relieved it was a dream and went back to sleep."

"When Commander Wilkins came in, lieutenant," Heimrich said. "That didn't wake you up?"

He saw Kelley hesitate, and gave him time. He could guess the thoughts of the sandy-haired man. They knew — they all knew by now — approximately the time Brinkley had been shot at. It would be interesting to see whether, now, Kelley remembered that his friend, and senior officer, had come at — at, say, twelve-thirty.

"No," Alan Kelley said. "He didn't wake me up."

So — once again, Commander Wilkins was on the loose, at a time when being on the loose might have significance. It might be, of course, that Wilkins was merely an unlucky man — in that, as in other things.

"I'm afraid," Heimrich said, "that I'll have to see Commander Wilkins. You want to ask him to come down, lieutenant?"

Kelley looked at Admiral Bennett. "Get him," Admiral Bennett said, and Kelley said, "Sir," and went.

They sat in the sun and waited. They heard Kelley climb the wooden stairs inside; heard him knock on a wooden door, and waited to hear him speak, be answered. But he did not speak. They heard him knock on another door, and heard, after a moment, the sound of a door closing. And then they heard Alan Kelley coming down the stairs again, and coming faster. He appeared in the doorway to the terrace and shook his head.

"Not there," he said, and said it needlessly.

Brady Wilkins had been in his room. He had slept in it. He was not there now, and not anywhere on the second floor. Once more, Lieutenant Commander Brady Wilkins was proving difficult to put a finger on — like a cricket.

Heimrich did what he could to fix the time of Commander Wilkins's departure. Dorcas had come downstairs a little before eight. Wilkins's door had been closed then, and she had assumed he was sleeping. She had walked carefully, so as not to waken him. Admiral Bennett had come down a few minutes later and thought the door had been closed, but had not especially noticed. Alan Kelley had been sleeping on a downstairs sofa when Dorcas came down. He had not, until then, heard anything to waken him. But, it appeared — it was said — that Wilkins had come in without waking Alan. It was obvious, then, that he could go out as quietly. It became, indeed, obvious that he had — unless Alan Kelley was lying.

So — although he had apparently been awake a good part of the night, Brady Wilkins had got up early and gone out quietly and — gone where?

"Captain," Dorcas said, "he's had — it's been a terrible thing for him. For all of us, but most of all for him, of course. He's — he's just gone walking somewhere or — or something. To be by himself."

That was quite possible, even quite likely. It resulted, nonetheless, in another absence when presence was desirable. Of course, during this period, nothing had happened. There was no special reason —

The telephone rang in the house. "Kelley," Admiral Bennett said, a little absently, and Alan said, "Sir," and went. He came back. He said, "For you, captain," and Heimrich went in and they heard him say, "Heimrich" and then, for some time, nothing more. Then they heard him say, as if he were very tired, "Damn," and then, "Yes. And — for Commander Wilkins too." He came back to the terrace. He stood and looked down at them.

"Professor Brinkley has disappeared," Heimrich said, and closed his eyes momentarily. He opened them. "Came to, apparently," he said. "Got out of the house without the trooper or the nurse seeing him — until it was too late. Drove off in a station wagon." He paused. "God knows where," he added.

Dorcas Cameron stood up. She said, *"Oh. The poor — the lamb!"* And then, after a moment, "But — he's *hurt!* What will happen to him?"

There was no answer to that, of course. The police were looking. They would find Walter Brinkley; it was to be hoped they would find him. It was to be hoped that, while careening around the countryside in a car — if that was what he was doing, and he had, apparently, started at a careening pace — nothing would happen to him. It was to be hoped that he

had fully come to, was fully himself. But —
that seemed very unlikely. Fully himself, Walter Brinkley was not, Heimrich thought, a man
to sneak — it must have come to that — out
of his own house; leave his own house as if
he were escaping from it.

Unless — several possibilities were apparent; none was particularly encouraging. In
some fashion, Professor Brinkley might have
been summoned. The trooper was sure nobody had telephoned; nobody got into the
house to summon the professor by word of
mouth, or to compel him. But the trooper had
been sure Brinkley was safe in bed, and that
coffee could be enjoyed at leisure. So had the
nurse, but she was not Heimrich's responsibility.

If not summoned — what? Had Brinkley,
coming out of hours of unconsciousness, not
only remembered what had happened but who
had made it happen? And gone off — not quite
himself, but thinking himself so — to capture
his assailant, bring him in? Had one idea, and
one only, in a still-fuddled mind?

He had been gone about half an hour when
Forniss telephoned Heimrich, from Brinkley's
house. The trooper had tried to get both of
them; had begun trying, apparently, just after
they had left the inn. Failing to reach either,
he had reported to headquarters. There

seemed to be nothing else he could have done — except, of course, to have been alert in the first place. It was too late to worry about that.

Brinkley on the loose — somewhere. And, once more, Wilkins on the loose somewhere. Heimrich didn't, he found, like any part of it.

"Heimrich," Admiral Bennett said, "Commander Wilkins had nothing to do with this. With any of this. You can take my word for that."

Heimrich only looked at him; wondered at apparently total faith, at the naiveté of that faith.

"Now admiral," Heimrich said. "I would like —"

And he stopped with that. Commander Wilkins — tall, black-haired, wearing a tennis shirt and walking shorts — came toward them; came up the path from "the place," and from the woods beyond it, the ravine beyond it. He walked stiffly and, when he was close enough, Heimrich could see the lined grimness of his face. Nobody said anything as Wilkins walked toward them, left the path and crossed the lawn toward the terrace. Nor did he, until he was almost at the terrace, seem to see any of them. But then he stopped and said, in a voice which rasped a little, "Oh.

Hello. You're here."

*"Brady,"* Dorcas said, anxiety in her voice. At that Brady Wilkins smiled a little — almost smiled.

"I'm all right, baby," he said. "Just —" But he stopped at that, as if he had forgotten what he had planned to say. He looked at the gun, resting across the arms of a terrace chair. Then he looked at Heimrich and, Heimrich thought, came back from wherever he had been.

"So," he said. "You found it."

"Did we?" Heimrich said. "It's your gun? The one you kept in the hall closet?"

Wilkins took two long strides across the terrace and looked down at the gun. He did not move to touch it.

"Could be," he said. "Probably is. They turn them out in thousands. But — same make, same model."

"Commander," Heimrich said, "I'd like to take your fingerprints."

"Oh," Wilkins said. "That way, is it? On the gun, I suppose? If it's my gun, I handled it. Not recently. Last time I cleaned it."

"When," Heimrich said, "you'd have wiped it off, wouldn't you?" He stood up. "I'd like your prints," he said again.

He got them. He looked at them. He compared them with the photographed prints. He put them with the other exhibits back in his pocket.

"Well?" Wilkins said.

"Yes," Heimrich said. "Commander, how did you know Beale was staying at the Maples Inn?"

"Who says —" Wilkins began and stopped.

"Yes," Heimrich said. "When you went there and asked for him. Tried to get him on the house telephone."

Wilkins had very cold eyes; now very level eyes. But, Heimrich thought, it was a strain for the man to keep them so. Under that coldness, that hard restraint, was Wilkins a seething man? Did he force a thin crust over violence?

"And," Wilkins said, "lie in wait for him. And — kill him? Why don't you ask it all at once?"

"All right," Heimrich said, "it's asked, commander."

"No," Wilkins said. There was no emphasis on the word, no violence in the tone. "I didn't kill him. Or — I suppose you want this too — my wife."

"Or," Heimrich said, "try to kill Professor Brinkley?"

"The professor?" Wilkins said. "Somebody tried to kill him?"

"Yes," Heimrich said.

"It's the first I've heard of it," Wilkins said. "So — it's the same answer."

"All right," Heimrich said. "Now — as to how you knew where to find Beale —"

"I didn't find him," Wilkins said.

"Look for him, then," Heimrich said. "You may as well sit down, commander. This may take time."

"With the light on my face, I suppose?" Wilkins said. "I don't have to answer anything."

"No," Heimrich said. "That's quite true, naturally. Only if you want to, commander."

Wilkins looked at him for a long moment, and Heimrich could read nothing in the cold eyes — not even what decision to expect. But then, abruptly, Wilkins sat down, and said, "Shoot."

"I have," Heimrich said. "Beale?"

"He —" Wilkins stopped and took a deep breath; the breath one takes in preparation for an ordeal. "He telephoned —" He paused again. "My wife," he said. "Saturday. Just before I got here. Before we went to the professor's party. She — she didn't tell me until the next morning."

He stopped once more. Heimrich waited.

"Beale said," Wilkins told Heimrich, and spoke carefully, slowly, "that he was in the neighborhood. On business. That he would like to stop by and — and say hello. She said no at first; that she didn't want to see him. But then —"

Then, as Lieutenant Commander Wilkins told it, speaking slowly and carefully, Conrad Beale had said that there was a little more to it than to say hello. Nothing that concerned Caroline Wilkins, really concerned her. Just — something he wanted to see her about. Again, nothing personal. Something that would help him in something he was working on. Something that wouldn't take five minutes. He would come any time that was convenient — any time within the next few days. He had told her that he was staying at the Maples Inn.

"Apparently," Wilkins said, "he told her something of a sob story. How much he needed help. I gather he didn't?"

"I don't know," Heimrich said. "She agreed to see him?"

Carry had — finally. She was always one to "help lame dogs over stiles." But she was doubtful about it — "upset."

"I told her she was making too much of it," Wilkins said. "Women see their former husbands all the time. And — I suppose I thought it would be a good thing, really, for her to see him again." He stopped; his face was bitter as, on the last words, his tone had been. "Brady Wilkins," he said. "The great psychologist."

Heimrich waited again.

"I told her," Wilkins said, his voice again steady, expressionless, "that sometimes things in the past — things that bother us, stick in our minds, even seem important — become — shadows when something happens to bring them up again. Seeing Beale again — I thought maybe — would serve — well, to put him out of her mind." He shook his head; for a moment he looked at the flags of the terrace, but not as if he saw them, or saw anything.

"Commander," Heimrich said, "she told him a time that would be convenient?"

"What?" Wilkins said, and seemed to be far away, and then to come back from far away. "Yes — Tuesday." Again he took a deep breath. "The day she was killed," he said. "The day she was killed." When he repeated the words it was as if he were, by repetition, making them real in his mind.

"Did he?" Heimrich said, and Wilkins looked at him and appeared to be puzzled, although that was hard to tell. But Wilkins spoke as a puzzled man might; he said he didn't get what Heimrich was talking about. That seemed a little unlikely, but Heimrich made it clear.

"Did Beale come here on the day your wife

was killed?" he asked, making it very clear indeed. "As you say was planned."

"How would I know?" Wilkins said. "I wasn't here. You know that."

Heimrich momentarily closed his eyes. He shook his head. He said that, no, he didn't know that.

"I have no idea where you were," Heimrich said. "It was difficult enough to get in touch with you the next day. You say you were on Long Island, but exactly where on Long Island seems to be a — a what? Defense secret? Long Island is a big island, commander. Montauk is one thing. Long Island City — a man could drive from here to Long Island City in — not much more than an hour. Or, here *from* Long Island City, naturally. It isn't as if you'd been in a rocket to the moon." Heimrich wondered momentarily why he had said that. Then he remembered Lieutenant Nelson. Mildly, he wondered where Nelson had got himself to.

"No," Wilkins said. "I wasn't here." His eyes narrowed. "You're getting at something," he said. "Some — accusation? You —"

"Now commander," Heimrich said. "Since you won't, or can't, prove where you were Tuesday. About noon, Tuesday, say. You say you weren't here. So — you couldn't have come on your wife and Beale together, could you? How do you want me to put it, commander? Not as — innocently together as she'd said they would be? Maybe you didn't really believe her when she told you that. Came back to check and —"

"*Heimrich,*" Admiral Bennett said. "We've had enough of this." His tone said, "That's an order, Heimrich."

It had, Heimrich supposed, been inevitable. An admiral does not willingly leave his command cabin. Heimrich looked at Bennett and was looked at. Commandingly, Heimrich supposed. Insubordination was to be put down. Perhaps even mutiny.

"No," Heimrich said, and was entirely mild of voice. "Not nearly enough, admiral. A woman has been killed. Your daughter — but for me it comes down to the killing. Murder. It will be the State of New York against — somebody. You're — sitting in on this, admiral, because I let you."

(And because a group so often helped; because, on a group, one can often play, letting a statement made by one lead to response from another; let action produce reaction.)

Admiral Bennett started to say something.

"No," Heimrich said. "It has nothing to do with you. If Commander Wilkins likes I can take him to White Plains. An assistant district attorney can talk to him. Ask him questions. The questions will be the same. It will merely be more inconvenient for everybody." He paused. "Well?" he said.

"You expect me to sit here," the admiral demanded — "sit here and listen to you accuse my daughter of — imply lies about her?"

Heimrich closed his eyes.

"Admiral," he said, "I don't really give a damn what you do. You can sit here. You can go somewhere and — play horseshoes. Or, Wilkins here and I can go to White Plains." He opened his eyes. "What it comes to," he said, "is, you're wasting my time. Everybody's time."

It looked very much like being an impasse, gray eyes and blue eyes locked, minds irretrievably in collision.

"Sir," Commander Brady Wilkins said, and Admiral Bennett looked at him, rather as if he were surprised to find him there.

"Well?" Bennett said.

"The captain didn't know her," Wilkins said. "He has to find things out. It's — got to be gone through, sir."

"No business —" the admiral began, but did not finish. He looked at Heimrich, who waited. "Carry on," Admiral Bennett said.

"Perhaps I can finish for you," Wilkins said. He spoke to Heimrich. His voice, Heimrich thought, was not as dead as it had been. His mind had wakened. Which might make it harder, might make it easier.

"Found them together," Wilkins said. "In a — what they call a compromising situation. Killed my wife with a shotgun. That's your theory, isn't it?"

"A possibility," Heimrich said. "The one I'm asking about."

"And — let Beale go?" Wilkins said. "Killed her and let him go?"

"Now commander," Heimrich said. "He may have had time to get away. Seen you coming and run for it. Perhaps they didn't even know you'd seen them. Perhaps your wife thought you hadn't. Pretended to be asleep."

Wilkins looked at him very steadily, for some moments.

"Captain," Wilkins said. "I don't think you believe a damn word of this."

"No?" Heimrich said. "You seem to be an intelligent man, commander. What's wrong with it? You kill your wife. Go looking for Beale. Find him and kill him, too."

"And then — take a shot at Professor Brinkley? I gather he was shot at, with that gun. Why?"

"From Brinkley's window, this house is in plain sight," Heimrich said. "Brinkley could have seen you arrive. Not thought anything of that, naturally. Perhaps not even have been sure it was you. Quite a distance for identification, and he hasn't seen you too often, has he? At the party, of course. Not often before that?"

"Once or twice," Wilkins said, but not as if he were thinking about that. His eyes narrowed. "Dropped a gun with my prints all over it?" he said. "Left it to be found?"

"No," Heimrich said. "Not all over it. Only one place — on the barrel, where you might have held it as you were carrying it. Wiped the gun off — with a handkerchief, perhaps. But then — slipped up. In a hurry. Jittery. Picked the gun up and carried it a few feet and dropped it again. Things like that happen quite often, commander. We find things like that a great help."

And again, Wilkins looked steadily at Heimrich, his eyes narrowed — and, Heimrich thought, his mind racing. Looking for an out? (Heimrich himself could think of several; wondered if Wilkins could.) Or — deciding which other way to go, and how far to go?

Dorcas Cameron was looking at Brady Wilkins, her eyes wide, her lips slightly parted. Alan Kelley lighted a cigarette, and the snap of his lighter was like an explosion on the sunny terrace.

"Well," Heimrich said, "why did you try to find Beale? If not to kill him?"

Wilkins did not answer immediately.

"Because," Heimrich said, and spoke very softly, "because you thought he had killed your wife?"

Would he go that way? That safer way?

"Captain," Wilkins said. "You make things so damn simple, don't you?"

"Now commander," Heimrich said. "Not unless they are. Well? Was that it?"

Slowly, Wilkins nodded his head, but it was not immediately clear whether he was saying it was that way or, unconsciously, pregesturing a decision reached in his own mind.

"I thought he might have," Wilkins said. "I — suppose that was it, really. I —"

He told it slowly, carefully. The care because he wanted to it right? Or because he did not want to tell too much?

The evening before — he checked, momentarily, on that, as if he thought it must be longer ago. The evening before, he had gone to the undertaking place and looked at a dead girl, lying horribly, in grisly simulation of life. He had sat for some time in the room where her body was. Then he had got up and gone out and back to the car — the car the Navy had provided. He had driven around for some time, and could not remember where, had not known where. He drove with the seat beside him empty — that was all he had really known.

And then, he had remembered Conrad Beale. Perhaps they wouldn't believe him, but he had not thought of Beale until that moment; not, actually, since Carry had told him of Beale's call.

"I asked you about him," Heimrich said.

Wilkins looked at him blankly. He said, "Did you? I don't remember."

"When you first got here," Heimrich said. "You said you had never seen him. You didn't say anything about this telephone call."

"I don't know," Wilkins said. "If you say so. I — all right, I wasn't thinking much then. Or — remembering much. You come back to — to a place that was always bright. And — she's dead. You go numb. Anyway, I guess I did. I suppose you don't believe that."

"Go ahead, commander," Heimrich said.

Whatever Heimrich thought, that was the first time he had really thought of Beale in — call it in context. He remembered, then, that Beale had been going to stop by and see Carry sometime. Then it had come to him clearly — sometime on Tuesday. *The day she was killed.* Then —

"I suppose," Brady Wilkins said, "I thought he might have seen something. Or — yes, that he might have killed her himself. I don't know now whether I really thought that or not. I couldn't think of any reason why he should but — well, maybe there was a reason I didn't know about."

He stopped then, momentarily. He looked at Admiral Bennett. But Bennett was not looking at him, was not looking at anything.

"It was — well, as if I'd come to," Wilkins said. "And I thought, You'd better go see this Beale. Find out what he knows." He stopped, he nodded his head, a little as if he had finished.

"It didn't occur to you," Heimrich said, "to come to us? To tell us that Beale might have been there?"

"No," Wilkins said. "I didn't think of that. Well —"

Heimrich already knew the rest of it. Wilkins had gone to the Maples Inn, asked for Beale, had him called in his room, got no answer. Then —

Once more he paused.

"That's all," he said. "I came back here. Not right away."

"No," Heimrich said, "I don't think so, commander. Not right away, certainly."

"Captain," Dorcas said. "Can't you see he's — told you everything?"

"No," Heimrich said. "Go on, commander. After you went out of the lobby of the inn — where you were seen, and knew you had been — then what?"

"I —" Wilkins said, and then fell silent.

"Went to his room," Heimrich told him. "Searched his room. And — what, commander? What did you find in his room?"

"Nothing," Wilkins said. "I —" He stopped. Unexpectedly, he shrugged his shoulders. "O.K.," he said. "I went to his room. I suppose somebody saw me?"

"It doesn't matter," Heimrich said, and by then that was true enough. "Why did you go? What did you expect to find in Beale's room?"

Abstractedly, Brady Wilkins rubbed a hand over his stiff black hair.

"You won't believe it, I suppose," he said. "But, I'm damned if I know. I — things still weren't very clear, I guess. I thought maybe —"

He had thought, he said, that perhaps Beale was in his room and had some reason of his own for not answering the telephone. He knew the room number, knew — from the fact that it was an even number — that it would be in the annex. He went out of the main building and along the walk to the annex. He had not, he said, made any particular effort not to be seen. He hadn't thought, however, that he had been seen. Apparently —

He looked at Heimrich in enquiry, and got no answer except, "Go on, commander."

He had found Beale's room and knocked on the door and then, he thought, called Beale's name. He was not really sure of this, he told them. He was sure that he had got no answer, either to the knocking or the calling.

"Then I thought," Wilkins said. "Damn it — I hardly know what I thought. That maybe there was something in the room — in his papers, I don't know what — that would help explain things. Show, anyway, what he wanted to see —" He stopped and swallowed. "See Carry about," he said, and the very lack of inflection in his voice was an inflection in it. "So, I went in."

"Not quite that," Heimrich said. "A little more than that, commander. Broke in. Forced your way in. I suppose you — just happened to be carrying tools?"

"Tools?" Wilkins repeated, as if the word were a new word. "Oh no, I used my knife. This —" He brought a big jackknife out of his pocket — a heavy knife, with heavy blades; a knife which was also a little nest of tools. "I tinker a good deal," Wilkins said. "The lock wasn't much of a lock."

"All right," Heimrich said. "You broke the lock — I agree it wasn't much of a lock. You went in. Beale wasn't there, I gather."

"No," Wilkins said. "I — looked around."

"You did indeed," Heimrich said. Then he leaned a little forward. *"And wore gloves, didn't you?* Gloves you just happened to have handy?"

"Captain," Dorcas said. "You're not being —"

"No, Miss Cameron?" Heimrich said. "Whoever killed Mrs. Wilkins wasn't being fair. Well, commander?"

"There's not much use in this, is there?" Wilkins said. "You figure you know all of it. Nice and neat and simple."

"The gloves?" Heimrich said.

"What's the use?" Wilkins said, but then, "All right. Yes. I did just happen to have them. Before I went to — to where she was — I changed. Put on a dark suit. One I hadn't worn since — oh, sometime in the winter. There was a pair of gloves in one of the pockets. A pretty thin story, isn't it?"

"Yes," Heimrich said. "And — you put them on, why? To keep your hands warm?"

(If a man under strain is taunted, a man may flare, lose control. If he is that kind of a man, has that kind of character; is a man who might, more greatly challenged — challenged on the dearest thing he knew — explode into violence. In short, into murder.)

There were arms on the chair Wilkins sat in. He moved suddenly, gripped the arms of the chair hard — so hard the knuckles of both hands whitened. His whole body tensed, as if he were about to come out of the chair. Then, slowly, as mind shouted orders to unwilling muscles — shouted them down, commanded them down — the gripping hands relaxed. Preparatory tenseness went out of the body.

"No," Wilkins said, in an entirely steady voice. "You're a very funny man, captain. But — no. So that I wouldn't leave prints. For your men to find if Beale raised a howl. Does that suit you, captain?"

"You didn't find anything? For all your looking? What were you looking for?"

"I told you. I don't know."

"Letters? That sort of thing?"

"Anything. I don't know what."

"Or," Heimrich said, "the gun? The gun used to kill your wife. Was that it? And — *didn't you find it?* Know then that Beale was the killer? And — *figure he'd come back?* Park his car in the lot? Get out of it under the light?"

"It's no use, is it?" Wilkins said. "No — and no and no. As many noes as you want. And won't listen to."

"Or," Heimrich said, "perhaps this, Wilkins?"

He took out of his pocket the photograph of a blocklike man, of a slender, pretty girl with a face which described nothing — of The Dutchman Schneider, and Opal Schneider, who had been Opal Potter. He held it out to Wilkins, who looked at it, and did not touch it.

"In his suitcase," Heimrich said. "If you looked at all thoroughly, you found it."

"All right," Wilkins said. "I found it. Looked at it. Put it back. It hadn't anything to do with us. With — Carry. Just an old picture of people I never saw before."

"Wilkins," Heimrich said, "was it *Beale* Professor Brinkley saw at the house that day? And — *did he tell you he'd seen Beale?* So that, when he heard Beale was dead, he'd come to me and say, 'Captain. This man Beale was around at about the time she was killed and *I told Commander Wilkins about it*'?"

"No," Wilkins said. The word came, seemingly, by a great effort.

"Did you realize that if he told us that you'd have had it? Did you put in a person-to-person call to him last night to find out whether he was home? Find out he wasn't and go there to — wait for him? The way you waited for Beale? And —"

"No," Wilkins said. "Oh — you can fit it together. I realize that. But — it's all wrong." He looked at Heimrich steadily. "All wrong," he repeated. "But that's no good, is it? Not good enough."

It wasn't, Heimrich thought. By all logic, denials — and the steadiness of eyes — weren't good enough. Why, then, the reluctance which was a shadow in his mind? Because Caroline Wilkins had been a girl with life stretching ahead, and seeming to stretch bright? Because Conrad Beale had been — what he evidently was, and a murderer to boot? Because, if one could stand off and judge, weigh value against value, Caroline and Brady Wilkins, singly or together, might be toted as outweighing a hundred Beales?

It is not for the police to stand off and judge. Heimrich, a policeman first, has often to do things he does not, as a man, want to do. He had to do one of them now. He stood up slowly.

"Commander Wilkins," he said, "I'm afraid I have to —"

He stopped. A big car came up the driveway. Paul Craig was driving it and his wife sat beside him. There was, Heimrich thought, a curious rigidity in their attitudes.

A plump man who seemed to be wearing a white turban was in the back seat of the big car.

# XV

Walter Brinkley, professor emeritus of English literature, got out of the car first. He got out a little awkwardly. He appeared to be wearing a bright yellow shirt, bright blue slacks and a tweed jacket — rather greenish in general effect — in addition to a white turban. He got out of the car awkwardly, it was apparent, because he had a revolver in his right hand and was pointing it at Mr. and Mrs. Paul Craig.

He opened the door on Margo Craig's side of the car — opened it politely — and Margo got out. She was tall and slender and entirely lovely and she wore walking shorts and a shirt but was, somewhat unexpectedly, barefoot. Professor Brinkley stood back a little, being careful — Heimrich observed — not to let the opened door come between him and the two who were, quite obviously, his captives. He waited for Paul Craig to get out, and Craig got out. He was wearing a terry cloth robe over swimming trunks, but he had canvas beach slippers on his feet. His face was as outraged as Captain Heimrich had ever seen a face.

Professor Brinkley waggled the gun slightly, indicating direction. Paul Craig and his wife, tall, straight people, walked toward the terrace. Margo walked uneasily, like a cat on wet ground. Gravel is injurious to bare feet. Craig's slippers slapped as he walked.

Professor Brinkley was much plumper behind them, and not nearly so tall, and was, of the three, the most oddly clothed. But a revolver, held ready, adds sufficently to stature.

None of the five on the terrace said anything. There did not seem to be anything to say.

Paul Craig was the first to speak. He slapped up onto the terrace and said, "Captain Heimrich. This preposterous behavior —"

"Scotch and water," Brinkley said. "I can't understand why it took me so long." He looked at Heimrich and shook his head. Then he blinked, as if it had hurt to shake his head. "Not in the least like Maryland," he said, with the air of a man who explains all. "But of course that was the Misses Monroe."

"Obviously," Margo Craig said, "the poor man is out of his mind."

It was, of course, as obvious as she said. A blow on the head had jarred Walter Brinkley's brain. It appeared that it had jarred it loose. Brinkley looked at Margo Craig and blinked again, and then, quickly, Dorcas was across the terrace and had her arms gently around the baffled little man. She defended; her look at Margo was close to a glare.

"Don't say that," Dorcas said. "It isn't that at all. He's —" She paused and held Brinkley to her as she might have held a child. "He's hurt," she said. "A little confused. It isn't fair to say —" She did not finish. She drew Brinkley to a chair and soothed him into it. "There," she said. "Don't listen to her."

"But that is precisely —" Brinkley began, but Craig did not wait for him.

"Then," Craig said, "you didn't send him, captain? I hardly thought you had, for all he said."

Heimrich shook his head.

"We were having breakfast on the terrace," Craig said. "He drove up. Early for a call, I thought. But Walter has often been — unconventional. I said something like, 'Morning, Walter,' and — he pulled a revolver out of his pocket. A *revolver*." It needed to be said twice to be believed once. "Said you wanted us. Forced us to drive here at —" He seemed to consider. "Gun point," he said.

"Miss Cameron, is right, of course," Heimrich said. "Mr. Brinkley was attacked last night. Injured his head. He's not supposed —"

"If," Brinkley said. "If you will listen." He

put the revolver down on the table in front of him. "People so seldom listen — really listen. At the party — my party — Mrs. Craig asked for scotch and water. I'm sorry, Paul, but there it is — scotch and *water*." And, as he used the word for the second time, its sound twisted oddly in his mouth. It was almost as if he had started to say "wagon" and changed his mind in mid-course.

"Of course," Brinkley said, and nodded his head slightly in agreement with himself, "I exaggerate somewhat. Nearer 'water,' actually." This time the sound was just perceptibly changed. "Much nearer," Brinkley said, and nodded his head again. A small man, round and pink of face, most strangely clad, with a bandage around his head and aware, Heimrich realized, of none of this — a teacher, making a point clear to a class he, probably, found a little backward.

"There," Dorcas said. "There, Mr. Brinkley. Just don't worry about —"

"One of the most difficult things to eliminate entirely," Brinkley said, explaining further. "Oh — 'dog,' perhaps. I'll grant you 'dog.' Particularly, it seems, for people from Kansas. Oh — northwestern Missouri, perhaps. And parts of Iowa." He granted them a section of Missouri, a part of Iowa. "But really indigenous, it seems, to Kansas. And certainly *not* indigenous to Maryland." His lecture ended abruptly. He looked at Craig. "I'm really sorry, Paul," he said.

"You damned well ought to be," Paul Craig said with asperity. "Coming at us with a gun in your —"

"Oh," Walter Brinkley said. "I had to do that. I didn't mean that. For — for finding out that Mrs. Craig doesn't really come from Maryland. Couldn't, you see. Anyone with an ear —"

"Captain Heimrich," Margo Craig said, and her voice was cool, each word as she continued shaped immaculately. "Do we have to listen to such preposterous statements from a man who, obviously, is —"

But she stopped. Heimrich was not looking at her. He was looking down at Brinkley and, although Heimrich said nothing, Brinkley nodded his head again. "Quite certain, captain," Brinkley said. "Certainly not Maryland. Almost certainly, Kansas. Rural, I'd imagine. Of course, so much of Kansas is."

"Yes," Heimrich said, and now he did turn to Margo Craig. "It is, isn't it — Opal Potter?"

He did not stress the name.

For an instant, Margo Craig's handsome eyes went blank. And then a strange thing happened to her face — it seemed to twist itself into another face, a very different face.

"You lousy copper," Margo Craig said, and her voice was no longer cool. Her voice had changed as much as her face had changed. "You and that crummy shakedown artist. That squealing punk." And — *her accent had changed.*

Paul Craig looked at his changed wife. He looked at her coldly, and his face was set harshly. Craig, Heimrich thought, after a quick glance at him, disapproves of his wife. That was it — that unquestionably was it. Paul Craig dismissed the changed woman with firm disapproval. And — that was all it was.

The glance was a mistake. He realized that as Margo Craig moved — moved with the quickness of a cat, struck out with her right hand almost as fast as a snake strikes. And — had Walter Brinkley's revolver in her hand. She backed away, then. Moved the gun slowly from side to side, showing what she could do with it.

"What do you *know?*" she said, and her voice was shrill. So — she was the one who cracked under tension. It was interesting to know; not, at the moment, particularly helpful to know. "The whole lousy bunch of you? How to say words nice. That's all. Dutch could have squashed the lot of you. Rubbed you out like he did a lot of punks. And laughed at a bunch of lousy cops. Like I'm doing."

But she was not laughing. She was screaming at them, and waving the revolver more
rapidly, gesturing with the revolver.

"Wrapped up in cotton," she said. "That
pretty-pretty wife of yours. The whole stink-
ing bunch of you. What the hell business was
it of hers? I worked like hell to bring it off
— and brought it off — and that better-than-
anybody bitch — what did she want to live
around here for? I — you'd better not, copper.
You're no different from the rest of them. Cop
or not I can shoot you full of holes — just
like the girl — and that double-crossing punk
of a Beale and —"

Heimrich moved. His hand came down in
a fist, aimed at the wrist. He was quick, and
knew he was not going to be quick enough.
No hand moves as fast as a bullet moves. He
could see her hand tighten on the revolver
and knew, here it comes, and I make a hell
of a big target —

She pressed the trigger.

And nothing happened. The hand came
down on the wrist and the revolver clattered
on the flagstones and Commander Wilkins,
nearest, moving the fastest, had it.

She tried to run, then — run barefooted
on biting gravel, toward the car. She did not
run far.

Held, she tried to fight free, and was lithe

300

and violent in Heimrich's hands, in Alan Kelley's hands. But it did her, of course, no good.

Nor, when she knew it was ended, did the words she screamed at them do her any good. Nobody tried to stop that, since it would do nobody any harm.

Through all this, Walter Brinkley sat listening intently and now and then nodding his head.

She ran out of breath.

"Definitely Kansas," Brinkley said. "A very characteristic accent." He nodded once more, confirming his certainty. Then he looked at the revolver in Commander Wilkins's hand.

"By the way," Walter Brinkley said, mildly. "That isn't loaded, you know. I never keep a loaded gun around the house. One never knows what might happen."

What Margo Craig had said before was nothing to what she said, screamed, when she heard that.

# XVI

As nearly as he could come to phrasing it, Walter Brinkley said, it had been as if he were having a dream. It — the thing in his mind — had had the disproportion, the raw immediacy of a dream. A bubble, if Heimrich liked, a bubble unpunctured by the rational mind. Brinkley digressed. He said that, when he had been a very young man, he had tried to write stories. "Before it became apparent that I was better at professing," he added, and smiled. During that time he had sometimes dreamed plots — dreamed them in full and fantastic detail. Sometimes he had wakened with such a plot, in all its carefully worked out absurdity, clear in his mind. Always, such plots had dissolved in the mind's reason. It had been as if this one did not.

They sat over drinks on the terrace of Walter Brinkley's house, and it was late Friday afternoon. Brinkley no longer wore his turban. A strip bandage did for that. Nor, of course, did he any longer wear a yellow pajama jacket and bright blue slacks.

Heimrich, with other things taken care of, for the time being, had come to congratulate

Walter Brinkley on going so straight to the heart of the matter and to find out how, not knowing at all where the heart lay, he had managed to do it. How, in short, had Brinkley realized the significance of Margo Craig's — Opal Potter's — State of birth. The answer was that Brinkley had not known it at all.

His conviction that Margo did not come, as she had said, had told Craig, from the State of Maryland, had seemed to him an entirely trivial discrepancy, even after he had managed to "localize" it, thanks to a casual remark of one of the Misses Monroe, made while discussing the weather, that the new Mrs. Craig was a Marylander by birth. An "unconsidered trifle," Walter Brinkley said, sipping a martini on his terrace. Something he might pass along to Heimrich when the occasion arose. Nothing, certainly, that he felt any urgency to pass along.

"Until I came out of it," he said. "Or — thought I had come out of it. With my wits addled. But then it had swelled up in my mind, become the one idea in my mind. Mrs. Craig was lying and she had to be made to admit it. It seemed of overpowering importance. As if it were that — only that — we had to prove."

"Well," Heimrich said, "as a matter of fact, it was. As important as you thought it."

"Dreamed," Brinkley said. "Not thought. Would you really have arrested Commander Wilkins?"

"Held for questioning, at least," Heimrich said. "A case could have been built up — had been. I can't say I liked it too well. Not the right character for the crime. However."

"She is?"

"Yes," Heimrich said. "She is. A violent woman, brought up in violence. Taught a violent way of life — and that only your *own*, what *you* want, matters. The Dutchman had a ready pupil."

"She's talked, I gather," Brinkley said.

"At length," Heimrich told him. "Almost without interruption, since she started on the terrace. She knows all the words. You'd be surprised."

"I doubt it," Brinkley said. "Harry?" Harry Washington appeared. He said, "Yassuh, professor, suh," really laying it on. Brinkley motioned toward the empty glasses.

"Now Walter," Heimrich said.

"Now Merton," Brinkley said, and Heimrich did not even wince, and Harry Washington — beaming, and laying the beam on also — went toward the bar.

"I know most of the words, actually," Brinkley said. "In an academic sense, perhaps. Because she'd made herself all over, of course.

And the — surface was cracked. Why Mrs. Wilkins? Because Mrs. Wilkins would recognize her as — as Opal Potter?"

"No," Heimrich said. "As Mary Evans. At the university — Missouri University. At least, Margo — seems simpler to call her that — assumed she would, since she herself recognized Caroline Wilkins when she saw her at your party. Whether Mrs. Wilkins would have —" He shrugged. "It's a human habit," he said, "to think of one's self as unique, essentially unchanging. Other people change. You don't."

"A point," Brinkley said. "Debatable, at least as regards many. But — a point. You think Mrs. Wilkins might, in fact, not have recognized her?"

"I don't know," Heimrich said. "She had certainly changed a lot — the picture of her with Schneider might be anyone — in fact, almost anyone *rather* than Margo Craig. Not only because of the changed hair color. The face — re-formed. But, Margo thought she would be recognized and, as you say, the surface would be cracked. And the whole structure would collapse."

"It began with Mrs. Wilkins, then," Brinkley said. "Not with this Beale?"

Harry brought drinks. Heimrich looked at his watch. Time enough, still.

It began, of course, with a farm girl in Kansas — a girl without parents, living with, and working for, distant relatives. On a run-down farm. Even in Kansas, farms do not always mean endless acres of wheat. A Cinderella, Heimrich supposed one could call her — if there were not already far too many "Cinderellas." A Cinderella with no ball to go to, nor any scheduled, and no prince. Unless The Dutchman was a Prince, and in a way he had been — a gangster guarding a load of liquor, holing up at the nearest place, the most inconspicuous farm, when — "Well," Heimrich said, "I suppose when a fix went sour." A gangster prince, but prince enough for Opal Potter's purposes.

"An unfortunate name," Brinkley said. "For a pretty girl to carry around. She must have been quite pretty."

Heimrich supposed so. Then marriage — Schneider apparently had scruples. Or, since Opal was not much more than a child, a sensible wariness of rape. Then school, and what she learned there, and, at the same time, what she learned from The Dutchman and his associates. "Which probably was plenty," Heimrich said. "Evidently was. Including the care and use of shotguns. She seems to have learned well."

"Intelligent, obviously," Brinkley said.

"This Schneider left her money and she used it to — probably 'better herself' is the term."

Intelligent, obviously. Intelligent enough to build a new person, learn — almost learn — to speak a new language. Make Opal Potter over into Mary Evans, college student; then into Margo Nowlin, daughter of a proud, if not peculiarly solvent, Maryland family. Finally, into Mrs. Paul Craig, equal to the best of North Wellwood — meeting, for example, the Misses Monroe.

"She would have been accepted?" Heimrich asked.

"Now captain," Brinkley said, and the words seemed faintly familiar to Heimrich, although he could not think precisely why. "Yes. North Wellwood is not — unassailable. And — the Craigs have been here for a long time." He shook his head, smiling at Heimrich. "You make too much of it, captain."

"Perhaps," Heimrich said. "As no doubt she did. But — doesn't Craig, Walter? And in a nicer way, the Misses Monroe?" Even you? Heimrich thought, but did not say.

"I don't," Brinkley said, "deny I know what you mean. She covered her tracks well, apparently?"

She had covered her tracks quite expertly — a trick Schneider, the whole of her early life, had taught her. She had, for example, used what remained of her money from Schneider to hire herself suitable parents, and a suitable sister. Which, admittedly, had thrown Heimrich off — led him to eliminate her as a possible Opal Potter.

"I had already decided the Schneider bit was more or less a side issue," Heimrich said, in self-extenuation.

Tracks covered, goal achieved — and then she found that a girl she had known in college was living only a few miles away. "A damn lousy break," Margo had said, when she was talking a lot. "Of all the damn lousy breaks."

She had decided to take action — not, she still insisted, the action of murder. Not that at first. She had gone to see Caroline Wilkins to find out "how much she wanted to keep her mouth shut." She had gone around noon on Tuesday.

"Yes," Heimrich said, in answer to an expression on Walter Brinkley's face. "That Mrs. Wilkins would want something, talk if she didn't get it — Margo accepted that implicitly. That's the way she thinks people are — all people. Schneider taught her that — Schneider and the rest."

She had gone with that intention, had knocked at the screen door of the Wilkins house, and not been answered, and had looked through it and seen, with the hall closet door not quite closed, a shotgun leaning in the closet corner. She still did not think of killing — said now she didn't. She remembered having heard something about a place, somewhere behind the house, where Dorcas and her cousin sun-bathed. She had gone in that direction, and found a path — and found Caroline sleeping.

And then she had remembered what she had just heard — what everybody had heard — about Old Ash Adams and the other girl, and had thought, "They don't squeal when they're dead," and gone back and got the gun. "It looked," she said, talking — talking far too much, but not being stopped — "like a perfect setup. They'd hang it on this crazy old coot." She had gone back for the gun and used it and got out, taking the gun. So that, when "they" started looking for a gun, they would find a wrong gun — preferably, of course, Ash Adams's gun.

"Her prints aren't on the gun, you say," Brinkley said.

"Now Walter," Heimrich said. "Ladies always wear gloves, you know."

Brinkley looked at him.

"All right," Heimrich said. "She thought so. One of the things she'd picked up along the way. Wear or carry. Like naval officers, incidentally. Oh, people pay undue attention to the little things. When they're not too sure. And you'll have to admit, the Monroe sisters do wear or carry."

"The commander's prints?"

"When you've cleaned a gun," Heimrich said, "you pick it up and put it where you keep it. Not, obviously, bothering about prints. In this case, in a corner of a hall closet."

Brinkley nodded.

So — Margo had Caroline taken care of. And then — Beale came into the picture. There they would have to guess, with Beale dead and Caroline Wilkins dead. Margo herself denied knowing how "the lousy little punk had got on to it." Heimrich himself supposed that Beale had seen a picture of Margo — one had been run, for example, in the *North Wellwood Advertiser* at the time of her marriage to one of North Wellwood's more distinguished residents. Beale might have seen such a picture, and seen through superficial changes and said to himself, "Margo Nowlin? The hell it is. That's Mary Evans at M.U., and before that it's Opal Potter Schneider and boy-oh-boy!"

He had — again this was an assumption — kept some track of Caroline Wilkins, his former wife — enough track to know that she, too, now lived in North Wellwood. He had gone to see Caroline — this was another guess, but a safe one — for corroboration — to find out whether she, too, had recognized a school-mate in masquerade. He had found Caroline dead.

"And that was corroboration," Heimrich said. "Plenty. He knew the kind of person Margo was, knowing her background. I imagine they thought pretty much alike. And now he really had something — not just a minor scandal: 'Gangster's Widow Makes New Life for Herself.' What he had now was worth real money. He went after it."

Exposure of the masquerade would have been bad enough — would have undone all Margo had worked for. That alone.

"Craig would have thrown her out," Heimrich said. "Because — she'd affronted him by lying to him. And, for other reasons. You agree, Walter?"

"Oh yes," Brinkley said. "I'm afraid so. Poor Paul."

That would have been bad enough; this, obviously, was worse. This might bring a murder charge. So — there was only one thing to do. Stall Beale until this setup, too, was right. Then, use the gun again. She did. "And," Heimrich said, "did her best to kill me in the bargain."

"And," Walter Brinkley said, "me. Why me?"

Heimrich considered briefly. There was no reason to tell his friend that he was, to Margo Craig, "that silly old fool." Editing was indicated.

"Having gone as far as she had," Heimrich said, "it was essential that she stay entirely free of suspicion. Any suspicion, any enquiry, would be fatal. Because, you see, Walter, her prints are on file. In Kansas City. As Opal Schneider, of course. No actual police record, no arrests. But — picked up for questioning once or twice, along with her husband. And, printed. Policemen like to keep a lot of records, you know."

"Yes," Brinkley said. "But, why me?"

"At the party," Heimrich said, "you talked a bit about regional accents. About the man on the radio. It — gave Mrs. Craig a headache."

Brinkley said, "Oh." He said, "But, I didn't then mean anything by it. Anything about her. It was just — I was riding a hobby. Probably, it gives a good many people a headache."

It had Margo Craig, at any rate. Not immediately — at least not a severe headache, immediately. "I decided nobody would pay any attention to the silly old fool," Margo had said, and Heimrich did not now repeat. But that had been when she thought she could brazen it out — if it ever did come up — before, leaving the party, she had seen Caroline arriving, and recognized her. When, further, it became a case of Murder One, Margo had decided that somebody might well believe the silly old fool — believe him enough, at any rate, to ask questions. She couldn't have questions asked.

"So," Heimrich said, "she put you next on her list. Called up, posing as a long lines operator, find out if you were home; found you weren't and went around to wait until you came. It had worked fine that way with Beale. Almost with you. But she missed."

"Not entirely," Walter Brinkley said and, reminded, uneasily changed position in his chair. "And left the gun, figuring she'd wound things up?"

Heimrich nodded.

"But," Brinkley said, "how would she know the commander's prints were on it?"

"She didn't," Heimrich said. "That was — call it a bonus. But — she knew *her* prints *weren't* on it. That was all that mattered. If anybody else had explaining to do, that was fine with her."

"I suppose so," Brinkley said. He finished his drink and looked at his empty glass. "It's too bad," Walter Brinkley said, "that Paul is such a — such a really hopeless snob. Poor Paul."

There are, Heimrich thought, a good many ways of looking at almost anything. In a sense, of course, his friend had, again, gone to the heart of the matter. If Opal Potter's long quest had brought her, in the end, to a different man — Well, it hadn't. Heimrich looked at his watch.

"Why not stay and have dinner?" Walter Brinkley asked. "Young Dorcas is coming over. And her boy, of course." Heimrich enquired with eyebrows. "Oh," Walter said, "she's quite all right now. At least — will be. Why not stay and see for yourself?"

"No," Heimrich said, and stood up. "Some other time, Walter. Tonight, there're some things I've got to do."

"Of course," Brinkley said, and stood up too. "I realize — things to wind up."

"In a sense," Heimrich said. "Actually — well, Walter, I've got a date with a dog. A very large dog. A Great Dane."

Brinkley looked at him. It was the first thing in all of it, Heimrich thought, which had really surprised this professor emeritus of English Literature.

"I will admit," Heimrich said, "the dog lives with a lady, Walter."

Walter Brinkley beamed at Heimrich and

walked with him to the car. He said that he would like to meet the lady. He said that, if sometime Heimrich would bring her to it, he would give another party.

The employees of THORNDIKE PRESS hope you have enjoyed this Large Print book. All our Large Print books are designed for easy reading — and they're made to last.

Other Thorndike Large Print books are available at your library, through selected bookstores, or directly from us. Suggestions for books you would like to see in Large Print are always welcome.

For more information about current and upcoming titles, please call or mail your name and address to:

THORNDIKE PRESS
PO Box 159
Thorndike, Maine 04986
800/223-6121
207/948-2962